THE LAST DAWN

HORIZONS

RICHARD C HALE

THREE THIRTY A.M. PUBLISHING

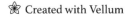 Created with Vellum

For Mallory

PART I

Michalla

&

A J

1

Michalla sighted through the rifle's scope and pulled the trigger.

The huge buck disappeared from view, the report of the gun echoing across the pasture and snow-filled forest. She took her eye away from the eyepiece and found the buck lying on its side. It kicked a few times and then lay still. She turned to A J and grinned. Talia, the big Labrador retriever bounded away from A J toward the deer.

"Nice," he said.

"You owe me."

He huffed and stood up from his prone position behind a rock. He brushed the snow from his thermal suit and slung his own rifle over his shoulder. She couldn't stop grinning as she joined him from her position behind a tree. They made their way the hundred yards or so to where the buck lay in the snow, its last dying breaths creating a mist around its head in the cold air. Talia paced around it anxiously, whining down in her throat. A few flakes of snow had started to fall, and Michalla looked up into the gray sky as A J finished him off with his knife.

"Talia! Come here, girl!" The dog bounded over to him, and he rubbed her coat. "This will feed a whole lot of people."

Michalla nodded, wondering if Marty and Harlee were having any luck on the section of the forest they were hunting. She hadn't heard a rifle report coming from their direction and figured they hadn't seen any game yet. Hopefully, they would get a good-sized deer as well.

The ARK didn't need the meat nearly as badly as Michalla needed to get out of the huge concrete bunker they had called home for the last three months. She and the rest of their little group had been unceremoniously dumped in the hills of North Dakota after the raid of the lab in south Florida. The same lab that had infected them all with the virus, or at least had tried to infect them all. Marty had been the only one to come down with it, but Dr. Thacker's serum had cured him of the disease that had killed the world.

And that's why they were here. Immunity and a cure for The Pukes. The surviving government of the United States had pretty much kidnapped them and brought them to The ARK to study them. And to understand why Dr. Thacker's serum worked. The underground bunker built into the side of a mountain here housed the acting president and his cabinet members and a select number of researchers, workers, and military personnel who would "rebuild" the country, and possibly the world. The fact that Michalla was pregnant made her even more special. Would the fetus survive?

Michalla unconsciously rubbed her growing belly through the suit that kept her warm in the frigid air and smiled at the feeling of her unborn child. At first, she had been horrified at the thought of carrying the monster's child and giving birth to a thing that would resemble him, reminding her every day of how it had come to be. But as the baby grew inside her, a maternal instinct began to take over, and she now thought of the child as only hers. Not the Ratman's. Well, her's and Marty's child. The close bond the two had formed after his brush with death from the virus had made Michalla feel an excitement at the thought of raising her own child and sharing the responsibility with someone she loved.

She smiled to herself at the thought of her being in love with Marty. Back when they first met, she would never have considered him in that way. He was just too different. But, that difference and his caring nature had ended up being what she loved the most about him. It hadn't happened overnight. It was more like a slow simmer, the beginnings of her feelings coming as she lay in the cell taking care of him as he suffered in the throws of the virus. He had seemed so helpless, yet strong and determined. Contradictory, but it was what it was. He was always a contradiction.

A J had set about field dressing the huge deer, and she shook herself from her thoughts and knelt to help, pulling her big knife from its sheath. As the heat escaped from the deer, it manifested in a cloud that hung over them and then drifted away.

The snow had started to come down harder as they worked and Michalla glanced up at the big flakes as the snowfall intensified. The weatherman back at The ARK had not forecast this amount of snow, and she wondered how heavy it would get. Of course, the weatherman in the bunker didn't have the tools that the modern weatherman had possessed before The Pukes, so it was usually just a good guess on his part. Without satellite imagery and a network of weather stations to gather data, they really had little to go on. But, as they worked, the clouds grew darker and heavier, and the snowfall intensified to the point it was dropping quite a bit of it around them. If it got any worse, it was going to be difficult to see and navigate their way home.

When they finished dressing the deer, A J unpacked the portable travois, and they hefted the deer up onto it, struggling with the weight. It was very heavy. A J grabbed one handle of the travois and her the other, and they started dragging the carcass down the hill toward where they had left their snowmobile. She struggled with the heaviness, and before long she was breathing hard with the exertion.

The snow was coming down in sheets now, visibility reduced to just a few feet, and Michalla struggled to get her bearings. A J stopped at one point and looked around.

"This all looks the same."

"I'm losing our tracks in the snowfall. It's covering them up." She searched around in front of her and saw what looked to be footprints to their left. She pointed. "There. That looks like them."

"Are you sure?"

"No." She sighed in frustration, turning around in a circle trying to find anything that looked familiar. The trees around her that she could see were obscured by the heavy snow, and the silence in the storm seemed to make things worse.

"Let's try and follow them and see where it leads," she finally said.

"Only for a little bit. I don't want to get lost in this."

They both knew that losing their way out here in this blinding snowstorm was a real possibility. The storm had come out of nowhere and was getting stronger by the minute. If it got any worse, it would be a complete whiteout, and then they'd be in real trouble. They might get trapped out here in the elements, and Michalla knew it could put them in real danger of freezing to death.

The cold was already seeping into her boots and gloves, her toes feeling numb and her fingers thick and stiff. They trudged through the deepening snow and cold and moved between the trees they could see with the deer carried between the two of them. Michalla started to feel a small bit of panic well up from within her, and she fought to push it down. The landscape had changed dramatically with the storm, and even though she didn't want to admit it, she had no idea where they were.

She took a step around a tree and lost her footing. She stumbled and then slid down a small rise and stopped just short of falling into a small creek. She didn't remember seeing any creek on the trek up the hill to the pasture. A J chased after her and knelt next to her.

"Are you all right?"

She nodded. "Yeah. I just slipped. Sorry."

He looked around. "I don't remember this creek."

"Me neither."

"We're heading in the wrong direction. We need to backtrack."

"I agree." She stood, brushed off the snow from her suit, and stood up straight, eyeing him. "I think we should leave the deer. It's too hard lugging it around, and we're lost. I think it's weighing us down."

"We need that meat. I agree it's difficult with it, but I really think we should try a little further and see if we find the snowmobile before we give up."

She didn't like it but nodded anyway. "Okay. A little more. But we're dumping it if we can't find the snowmobile."

She looked around her at the heavy snowfall. It seemed like it had gotten worse in just a few minutes down here by the creek. She couldn't see anything but A J right in front of her and the small creek at her feet. No trees. No terrain. Nothing but the tracks right in front of her that disappeared into the white.

"Come on," A J said and led the way, stepping in his own tracks and finding the travois again.

She picked up her handle, and they turned it around heading back the way they had come. These fresh tracks were easy to see, but as soon as they arrived at the point where they had taken the turn, everything melted into the whiteness. She pointed to her left, and A J nodded. They headed in that direction, looking for signs of their previous path up here, but having little luck finding it. A J pushed on anyway, and after about ten minutes, she stopped him again.

"We're lost."

"We're not. Not yet. Just a little bit turned around. We'll find the snowmobile."

He turned to his right and left, but she could tell he could see no better than her. Everything was white. She held up her hand in front of her face and was amazed at how it even seemed faded. The heavy snowfall seemed to deaden sound as well, and the only thing she could hear was the steady beat of her heart in her ears, and a gentle shushing of the snow falling past her face. It was eerie and surreal.

He pushed on ahead, dragging his handle as she kept pace with him, dragging her own side. After five more minutes, she stopped again.

"We need to abandon the deer." She looked at him hard.

He sighed, glanced around again as if looking for someone to help them decide, and then he focused on her face. "Yeah. You're right. Let's get it off the travois and pack it back up into my pack."

They shoved the carcass off the travois, and he folded it up, stowing it in his backpack. He shrugged the heavy pack back onto his shoulders and looked once more at the dead deer lying in the snow. The snow had already partially obscured it in only a few minutes. Michalla realized then that they could possibly have walked right past the snowmobile, seeing only the snow that covered it. It would look like any other boulder or shrub shrouded in snow.

She looked around, trying to find Talia, but the dog had disappeared. She was sure she was much better equipped at finding her way around in the storm just by scent, but she still worried the big dog would somehow get lost.

"When is the last time you saw Talia?" she asked.

"About ten minutes ago. I saw her move past us and then she faded into the snow."

"Do you think she's lost?"

"Nah. That dog could find her way out of a total blackout."

"But this is looking like a whiteout."

"Same thing."

"I don't know..."

"She'll be fine. Come on."

He headed out again, and she followed glancing one last time at the deer carcass. She hoped they'd be able to retrieve it after the storm before scavengers found it. The cold should keep it in good shape.

They trekked through the deepening snow, A J focussing on the ground trying to find their old tracks, but she could see nothing in the snow. Every hump and ridge and bump looked the same, and she didn't know a footstep from a branch under the thick blanket that was growing thicker by the second.

Talia barked up ahead, a weird sound like her deep voice was inside a bale of hay or some cotton. Michalla stopped, and tried to find where it came from, but felt disoriented as she looked around in the almost complete whiteout. A J had not stopped, and he faded into the whiteness in a matter of seconds. She caught up quickly, the fear of getting separated from him settling in the pit of her stomach.

Talia bounded out of the whiteness and went up to A J, her coat covered in a layer of snow that had not yet melted. He brushed it off of her and rubbed her sides.

"Where did you go, girl? Did you find the snowmobile?"

Michalla stepped to the dog and patted her head. "Stay with us. I don't want to lose you in this."

Talia only wagged her tail and then shot off again up ahead before she could grab her. They stepped to her tracks, and A J followed them. Maybe she had found the snowmobile. Talia seemed like the best thing to follow at the moment as they really had no other choice.

After another five minutes, A J stumbled and went down. He started to laugh. She went to him.

"Are you all right?"

"Yeah. Found the snowmobile." He patted a hump of snow next to him, and she heard the hollow sound of his hand hitting the fiberglass body. Green paint showed through where his hand had brushed the snow off.

"Oh, thank God," she said.

She moved to it and started sweeping the thick layer of snow off of the seat and top, exposing the whole vehicle. If they had been two feet to either side, they would have walked right past it.

A J stood up and tried the ignition. It started right up, the engine idling noisily in the snow.

"At least it works," A J said.

Talia appeared again from their left and paced in front of them. She sniffed the ground and then waited. She didn't seem worried about the storm one bit; in fact, she seemed happy to play in it.

A J climbed up on the snowmobile, and Michalla slipped in behind him, wrapping her arms around his waist.

"Come on, girl!" she said. "Hop on up here."

She patted the seat behind her and Talia leaped up. A J put the snowmobile in gear and turned it around, so they were headed in the right direction.

"Go slow," Michalla said. "I can't see a thing."

"Yes, Mom."

"Shut up."

"Yes, Mom."

She whacked him on the back but was glad he was in a joking mood. It had been pretty serious for a while. She felt a bit better now. Cold, but better.

AJ gave the snowmobile some gas, and they got moving. He did his best to stay on the path, but with the visibility down to a few inches, it was difficult at best. He'd wander off to the left or right and find a tree appearing directly in front of them out of the white. He'd turn hard to go around or even back up and start again. He was doing his best, but Michalla now worried they'd wander off the path and end up in the middle of the woods hopelessly lost.

Michalla's teeth chattered as the cold seeped in even through the thermal suit. Her fingers and toes were numb, and she hoped she wasn't getting frostbite. The temperature seemed to be dropping as the storm intensified and she knew from experience that this was more than likely a big front that would drop in behind the precipitation. The only real question was how cold it would get and how fast.

Talia grew tired of riding and jumped off after a few minutes. Michalla watched to make sure she was following and was relieved to see her keeping pace with the machine.

They made slow time along the path, and after about thirty minutes, the storm intensified even more and became a complete whiteout. AJ stopped and turned around.

"I can't see a thing!" he shouted. "I'm afraid I'll get us lost."

"We don't have a choice. It's either take our chances and hope we make it back or find a place to shelter until this is over. I don't see any places to shelter."

"I don't see anything."

"Keep going slow. I trust you."

He shook his head and started forward again. She knew he was doing his best, and she didn't think that she could maneuver the snowmobile any better than he was doing. They'd just have to feel their way along the path and hope for the best.

She let her hand fall to her belly and rubbed at the small bump, hoping her unborn child would forgive her for what she was putting him or her through. She worried about the cold and the ride and everything that could go wrong. She was about to tell A J to go even slower, when the snowmobile lurched, sagged to her left, and then dropped sideways as they careened over some edge. She cried out and was thrown from the vehicle as it tipped over. She fell hard and rolled down a steep embankment and then everything went blank as she struck something hard.

2

Marty pushed through the deepening snow, the blizzard in full swing now as the visibility deteriorated to only a few feet in front of him. Harlee trudged right behind him, her heavy breathing the only sound beside their footsteps in the white world that was their reality.

Their snowmobile had broken down over a mile back, and they had had to trek the final distance on foot with a huge blizzard raging. The storm had started off slow and then built to what he now would call a whiteout. The swirling snow and deepening cold made him more cautious as he "felt" his way along the path to The ARK.

"Are we almost there?" Harlee asked from behind him.

"Not too much farther. How're you holding up?"

"I'm freezing. Even my butt. Especially my butt."

He chuckled, but then he realized she was serious. "Want me to rub it?"

"You wish." She finally smiled at him. "I'm gonna tell your girlfriend you were hitting on me."

"Survival. That's all it was. Survival in the cold."

"Perv."

Just as he was about to stop and check his position, the south entrance to The ARK loomed up out of the white, and he breathed a sigh of relief. He pointed.

"Thank God," Harlee said. "I want hot chocolate."

"I bet A J will have it waiting for you."

"He better."

Marty pushed the door open and stepped into the warmth of The ARK, the lone sentinel standing by the watch desk. Sergeant Hector Wilton looked up and then walked over to help them get out of their gear. Marty stamped his feet off and removed his gloves as the warm air felt good in his lungs. He grinned at Hector.

"It sucks big time out there."

"I'm sure it does. You guys are late. All of you are." Hector looked them up and down, his knowing eye looking their suits over for any sign of damage.

"Our snowmobile broke down about a mile out. We had to leave it on the path."

"Our equipment is old. I'm surprised it hasn't left you guys stranded until now."

"You said, 'All of you are.' Where's Michalla and A J?"

"Haven't returned."

"Are you serious? I would have thought they would beat us back no problem."

"As serious as can be in this weather. This caught everybody by surprise."

"Has anybody gone out looking for them?" Harlee asked.

"The order from the Colonel is that no one is to leave The ARK. No one."

Marty was in the process of removing his boots when he stopped and looked up at Hector. He started to put them back on.

"Then you didn't see us, Sergeant. I'm going back out to look for them."

"You are not."

"I am. Are you going to stop me?"

"We all have our orders. Not only will you be endangering yourself, but also Michalla and A J. They've been trained to survive in conditions like this. I'm sure they're probably hunkered down somewhere riding this storm out, a nice fire going to keep them warm and cover over their heads to keep them out of the conditions."

"I don't agree." He slipped his gloves back on and made to move toward the door. Harlee did the same.

"I'm going too."

"Wait!" Hector said. He looked them over, then turned and went to the cabinet behind him. He pulled open a drawer and pulled two sets of snow goggles out. He handed them each their own. "Take these if you insist on going out. They'll help with the whiteout."

"Thanks."

"I didn't see you."

"You didn't see us." Marty grinned at him and then clapped him on the back. "We'll be back before nightfall with them."

"You better. I'm not coming out looking for you if you're not."

"I figured as much. If we're not back, we're either dead or hunkered down ourselves."

Marty opened the door, and the snow swirled in with the cold.

"Good luck," Hector said.

"I think we're going to need it," Marty said. He stepped out into the cold and put the goggles on. The storm had grown even worse in just the few minutes they had been inside.

"I can't see crap," Harlee said next to him.

"You can stay."

"No way."

"Put your goggles on. It helps."

She slipped them over her face and eyes and looked around. "Liar."

He shook his head and headed back down the path. If Michalla and A J were lost, it was going to be almost impossible to find them in this.

But, he had to try.

~

MICHALLA FELT wetness on her face and opened her eyes. Talia breathed warmly on her skin and licked her again, whining. She pushed the dog away.

"Get back, Talia. Your breath is horrible!"

Michalla found herself on her side, her back up against a tree, the cold seeping into her joints. The snow fell so hard she could hardly see in front of her. The memory of the snowmobile tipping her off of it as it fell down some kind of ravine flooded back into her head, and she sat up quickly. A pain in her shoulder stabbed into her body, and she reached up to feel her suit. It was intact, and she wiggled the shoulder, feeling the pain ease off. She didn't think anything was broken.

Talia moved away and disappeared into the whiteness as Michalla stood, trying to get her bearings. She was on some kind of hill, her footing precarious as she steadied herself against the tree. She couldn't see the snowmobile or A J.

"A J! A J! Where are you?"

She thought she heard something to her left and she turned and took a few tentative steps down the hill. The overturned snowmobile appeared in front of her, a small cloud of steam coming up from the engine. It was still hot, so she must not have been out long. She circled around it, but A J was nowhere to be seen.

"A J! Can you hear me?!"

She listened closely and could barely make out his voice.

"A J! Shout out to me so I can find you!"

His voice came louder from down the hill, and she moved quickly toward it. He shouted her name and then heard Talia barking. She slipped and slid down the hill, her hands clawing at anything to stop her. She struck another tree and came to rest up against it. A J spoke from right next to her.

"Hey."

She turned and found his face a foot or so away. She crawled to him.

"Are you all right?"

"I think my leg is broken." He sucked air in through his teeth as he tried to move it, and then cried out. "Yeah. It's definitely broken."

She looked him over and could tell that the leg looked funny even through the thermal suit. She wouldn't risk removing the suit to look more closely.

"It doesn't look good," she said.

"It hurts like a mother."

"Can you stand?"

"I don't know. Help me up."

She stood and tried to pull him up, but he fell back, the pain clearly evident on his face. He reached for her again, and she was able to help him up to stand on one leg.

"I'm up."

She smiled at him. "You are. Let's try and get you moving."

He clutched her around the shoulders tightly, and she started to move down the hill. He limped on one foot, trying his best to move with her.

"We're going in the wrong direction," he said.

"I don't think I can move you uphill. We can only go downhill."

"Downhill to what, though?"

"Something that's not so exposed. Our options are few. You can't make it back up the hill with just me helping, and we can't stay out here in this storm without freezing to death. We look for shelter, or I build a snow shelter, and we hunker down inside it until the storm passes."

"Okay."

She started moving again, Talia keeping pace with them as if this was all in a day's work and nothing was wrong. Michalla loved the fact the dog could always look at the bright side.

The ground began to level off, and she worked her way around trees, keeping her eyes open for anything that would work as some kind of shelter. A fallen tree, a cave, some rocks, anything to get them out of the wind and blizzard.

"I have to rest," he said.

She let him sink down to sit against a tree, and she looked around, the snow falling harder and her vision down to a foot at best. Talia moved in and out of her sight, but she didn't call her back. The dog seemed to be able to find her way around in this storm without a problem.

"I'm going to look around some more. I won't be gone long."

"Don't get lost," he said.

"I can still see my own footprints. As long as I keep the distance short, the prints shouldn't have time to fill up with snow before I get back."

He nodded and made a pained face again as he shifted trying to get comfortable. His teeth chattered in the cold, and she knew he must be going into shock. She had to find something soon. He could go into hypothermia at this point, even in the thermal suit.

She moved off to her left, moving in between the trees and small rocks. The ground seemed to be mostly level here, and she decided it was the best option to find something. Or maybe along where the ravine started to rise back up toward the path they had veered off of.

After ten minutes, she was about to give up, turning back

toward where she had come to make sure she could see her trail. A small dark patch appeared in her peripheral vision, and she moved toward it. As she got closer, it grew into the mouth of a small cave. She ran up to it, excited, and bent down to see inside.

It was dark and hard to see, but it felt deeper than it looked. She pulled out her flashlight from her backpack and shone the beam into the opening. The walls of the cave were about ten feet wide on both sides, and at the back, it turned off to the right and disappeared into the side of the hill. It must be deeper than she could see. She hoped it was empty.

She shut the flashlight off and followed her own tracks back to A J. She found him against the tree with his eyes closed. A brief panic welled up inside her and then he opened his eyes and looked at her.

"You're back. I was getting worried."

"I found a cave."

"Is it good?"

"It's almost perfect. Big enough for both of us and Talia inside. Let's get you to it, and I'll start a fire inside to warm us up."

He reached up for her, and she helped him painfully to his feet. She walked him toward the cave, and he did pretty well considering he was only able to use one leg. Talia appeared again out of the whiteness and stayed with them. It seemed she knew she needed to stay.

At the cave opening, she took out her flashlight again and let A J sink to his knees. They would have to crawl to get in, and she hoped he'd be able to do that with his broken leg. He cried out once as he moved inside, but was able to make it favoring his good leg. She handed him the flashlight after he'd found a spot sitting up against the wall.

"I'll go find firewood."

He nodded. "I can't believe this is here."

"Somebody is looking out for us." She smiled and then turned to look for some wood.

It was hard searching in the deep snow, but she found sticks and branches poking up out of the whiteness and collected a pretty good stack in about twenty minutes. She made her way back to the cave and pushed the sticks in front of her as she crawled inside. She found him where she'd left him, his eyes huge in the dimness of the flashlight.

She set about making a fire, and after several attempts at striking the lighter with her gloved hands, she finally pulled them off and was able to make her fingers work despite the fact they felt like small blocks of ice. As the little flame grew in the tinder into a bigger fire, she held her hands up to the warmth and breathed a sigh of relief.

"Fire going," she said.

"It feels good," A J said as he scooted a bit closer to it.

She kept her hands up by the fire and slowly feeling returned to them, a not-so-pleasant tingling making her feel relief that she hadn't suffered any frostbite that she could see. She went to him and pulled his gloves off checking his fingers for any signs of frostbite. A J's hands looked fine.

"You're good," she said, scooting back to her side of the fire.

The cave warmed slowly, and she dug in her backpack for the energy bars she knew she had. She found two and handed one to A J.

"I'm not hungry," he said. "In fact, I'm a little nauseous."

"It's the shock. Do you feel sleepy?"

"Yeah. I can hardly keep my eyes open."

She nodded. "Rest. I'll keep an eye on you."

"What's going to happen to me?"

"We're going to get you out of here as soon as this storm lets up. If we have to spend the night in here, we'll be fine. I can gather more wood in a bit to hold us over if need be. I think we have a couple hours of daylight left."

"You should leave me. I don't want something happening to you because of me."

"I'm not leaving you. You wouldn't leave me, right?"

She watched him think about it, and she grinned at him. "Right?"

He finally smiled. "Of course, I wouldn't."

"I'm not going anywhere. I have to keep you safe until help can get you up out of this ravine and back to The ARK."

He shifted a bit, trying to find a more comfortable spot on the dirt floor. He looked up into her eyes.

"Thank you."

"A J..."

"We look out for each other. We have since we met. I don't ever want that to change."

"It won't. Now, rest. And stop getting all mushy on me. That worries me more. You're going to be fine."

"Okay."

He closed his eyes, and she watched his breathing slow, and then he fell asleep. She sighed, added another stick to the fire, and munched on her energy bar. She knew they would survive this. They just had to stick to what they had learned and keep warm.

3

Marty stared up at the ceiling and closed his eyes.

Sleep wouldn't come. After hours of tossing and turning in the queen bed that he and Michalla shared, he couldn't find sleep. Not with her still out there somewhere in the freezing storm.

He and Harlee had searched until it grew dark, the storm so intense they could hardly see a foot in front of them. The last running snowmobile hadn't let them down, but it had been impossible searching out there as the storm raged on. They'd stopped periodically, shutting the engine down and shouting their names, but nobody had answered, and they had seen no sign of them on the path or anywhere they had looked. The pasture where they'd been hunting was a complete whiteout, and there was no sign of their snowmobile or them. Marty and Harlee had returned to the south entrance of The ARK defeated and worried. They had promised Hector that they would return before dark and they knew it would be his ass if they had not obeyed. Still, it had been hard to abandon the search for the night.

Marty sat up, rubbed his hands across his face, and stood

up. The little room that he and Michalla called home was just that. A little room barely big enough for one. But it was all they had. The ARK was not a resort or huge place that could house everyone in style and comfort. It was a place for survival. A place to hunker down in hiding for however long it took for the world to be safe again.

It had been primarily a place to shelter from the atomic apocalypse that never came, but when the pandemic hit, it had been transformed into something that could be utilized without much refitting. The virus had struck so fast and with such ferocity that there hadn't been time to change it much anyway. The one hundred and fifty or so occupants that lived in The ARK had come to call it home in the past few months and were grateful for the shelter and safety it provided. The acting government that survived the plague now ran what could still be called The United States of America from within these walls, but for the most part, the rest of the country was on its own.

The room held a queen-sized bed, a couch, a small TV that was never turned on, a sink, a hotplate, a microwave, and a shower and toilet in what amounted to a closet. Michalla had added a picture she had found down in the storerooms and a colorful throw over the end of the bed to add a little life to the gray, stale, walls.

Marty looked at the empty bed, the bed that he and Michalla shared, and felt a pang of regret fill his chest. He should be out there. Right now. Searching for her no matter what the conditions. She had been there for him on more than one occasion. Without question. She had stayed at his side in that jail cell of a lab back in Florida. As the virus raged through his body and then as the serum that Dr. Thacker had developed did its thing to combat it. She had stayed with him through it all.

And when the panic attacks hit him down deep in The ARK

—the attacks that came as his imagination ran wild with thoughts of all those tons of rock and earth above his head pressed down on him stealing his breath—all he could do was lay there in a fetal position as Michalla held him and comforted him until the attack passed. He looked up at the ceiling, that familiar feeling of panic beginning to well up from inside him, and he pinched the inside of his wrist until it hurt. Slowly, his breath came back, and the feelings left him.

She had helped him gain control of those feelings, and for that, he had been eternally thankful.

Enough. He couldn't wait here any longer. He'd fight whoever he had to to get back to searching for her and A J.

He grabbed up his boots, slipped them on, and left the tiny room. As he walked the dimly lit quiet hall—more like a tunnel —the sounds of his boots echoed across the concrete. The rest of The ARK was silent in sleep. He pressed the button for the elevator, and the doors opened immediately, the small car waiting for him as the fluorescent light in the ceiling of the car flickered.

As the elevator creaked and moaned during its ascent from deep within the mountain, the feeling of claustrophobia crept in again, and he repeated the pinching process at his wrist. He closed his eyes, took slow deep breaths, and found that he could manage the panic that welled up from within. The elevator dinged, and the doors slid open much to his relief. He stepped from the elevator and looked up at the one working clock in the facility.

2:30 a.m.

Damn. It was still the middle of the night. He had hoped that time had somehow marched on much faster than it had felt cooped up in his room. But it had not. He sighed and headed for the south entrance.

The upper levels of The ARK were deserted at this hour. There was supposed to be a sentry around here somewhere, but he could be off doing his rounds or maybe even asleep somewhere in the space, hidden from anyone who might notice. In the prep room to the south door, he pulled a thermal suit off of the rack and began dressing. A knitted cap and heavy-duty gloves completed his ensemble, and he pushed the door open to the night.

It was cold. Bitterly cold. If he had to guess he'd say it was zero or a negative number. Nobody stopped him or asked him where he was going so he moved toward the motor pool and hoped he'd have the same luck. But when he heard metallic clinking and tools being dropped, he knew that Roland McAuley, one of the mechanics who worked on all the vehicles, would be up and busy as the rest of The ARK slept.

He stepped to the snowmobile that Roland was working on and said, "Morning."

Roland jumped and dropped the wrench he had been using on the engine.

"Holy crap, you scared the shit out of me," Roland said, looking around as if he expected a crowd to be standing in front of him.

"Sorry. I guess you're used to being alone this late."

"Is it late? I'd call it early. Marty, right?"

"Yeah."

"What are you doing up? Couldn't sleep?"

"Something like that."

"You're the dude who's with the girl that's missing. Michalla." A statement, not a question.

"That's me."

"Has to be hard. Worrying about her out there in the cold. And man, it's cold right now." He rubbed his hands together and then grabbed his pair of gloves and slipped them back on now that he wasn't working.

"It is. And that's why I'm here. I want to take one of the snowmobiles and start looking again."

"You know they don't allow night ops."

Marty nodded. "I know. But I would think they'd make an exception for this case. I mean Michalla and A J's lives are on the line. What if she's hurt and can't get to a shelter or make one?"

"I hear you. If it were me, I'd let you go, but..."

"It is you. You're the only one here. Listen, I'll only take it until dawn. Then I'll have it back, and nobody will have to know but you and I."

"I don't know. It's my ass if something happens to you out there as well."

"The storm is over. It's clear as can be, so I can see perfectly with one of the big lanterns. I'll stay to the path with the snowmobile. Come on, Roland. Think if it was your wife out there. What would you do?"

"I'm not married."

"You know what I mean."

"She's not your wife, either. "

"Not yet."

Roland seemed to make up his mind. He walked over to the key rack and pulled the snowmobile key down and brought it over to him.

"It's the only one left that's running," he said. "Don't screw it up."

"I won't. I promise. Thanks, buddy. I owe you for this."

"You do. Be back before dawn or it's both of our asses."

"I will."

Marty took the key from him and went to the supply cabinet and grabbed one of the big spotlight lanterns on the shelf. He hopped onto the snowmobile and started it up. It cranked right away and idled smoothly beneath him. He turned it toward the path and gave it gas, accelerating smoothly away into the dark.

He felt there was a good chance he would find her. Something that just felt right. He turned on the big light and began searching the woods on either side of the path.

MICHALLA SAT up quickly in the low light and looked around. Something had woken her. Talia was awake as well, and a low growl rumbled down deep inside her. Then the dog stood up and growled louder, waking A J.

"What?" A J mumbled as he came awake.

"Shh," Michalla said. "Something is out there," she whispered, and A J turned to the entrance of the cave. He tried to get Talia to sit, but she wouldn't.

Some shuffling noises came to them from outside the mouth of the cave, and Michalla grabbed up her rifle. She held it ready as Talia continued to growl. A low rumble came from outside the cave, and then a black muzzle appeared as the bear pushed inside the entrance. Talia went crazy and started barking furiously as the bear roared at her. A J grabbed up a stick from the fire and pushed it toward the bear, the flame clearly bright in its face. It made a weird mewling noise in its throat and then pulled back out of the cave entrance. Talia chased after it.

"No! Talia, no!" A J shouted, but the dog didn't listen.

They heard her barking and growling at it outside and then Talia ran off chasing it. Michalla looked at A J and saw the fear in his eyes.

"She'll be okay," Michalla said. "She's agile. She'll be able to out-maneuver whatever that bear tries."

"I don't know. I hope she doesn't try and attack it."

They listened for a few minutes, and Talia's barking grew farther and farther away until it faded out completely. A J looked over at Michalla.

"She'll be fine," Michalla said. "How are you feeling?"

"Hurting pretty bad."

"I have some pain pills. I should have given them to you earlier, but when I finally thought of them you were asleep, and I didn't want to wake you."

"I'll be fine."

"Just take one. It will help you to sleep."

He seemed to think about it for a second and then nodded his head. She fished around in her backpack and came out with a pill. She handed it to him, and he swallowed it with some water.

"Feel better already."

She laughed. "It won't work that fast, dummy."

"Maybe it's the thought of some relief that makes me feel better."

"Do you want two? You can have two if you want."

"No. Let's see how this does."

Talia came back in, panting, her coat covered in snow. A J inspected her and found nothing wrong. She sat next to him as he rubbed her sides. She had a look that said, "I'm a badass," and Michalla smiled at the dog. She wondered how she came up with such things in her head.

She rubbed her belly and felt the small little miracle growing inside her move beneath her hand. It was always an amazing feeling when the baby shifted or moved. Even at this early stage in her pregnancy.

The doctors at The ARK monitored her closely and were encouraging in their words that her pregnancy was progressing along without a hitch. She was young, healthy, and active, and they expected things to go normally and naturally. She couldn't wait to meet her child; all negative thoughts of the Ratman and what he'd done to her were pushed to the back of her mind. With Marty, she felt that she could have a happy life and love this baby with all her heart. Such a big change from when she first realized she was pregnant, but she figured it was natural for a mother to love their child no matter what, and that some hormonal changes within her were fueling the motherly instinct that was raging within her.

She added another small log to the fire, stoked it to get it burning brighter, and relished the warmth it put off. She glanced over at A J where Talia lay up against him staring at her and saw that he was asleep again. The pill seemed to be doing its job. She lay down and stared up at the ceiling above her head and thought of Marty. Was he worried about her? Would he do something foolish and come looking for her in these conditions? Would he risk injury to find her or something even worse? She hoped not. She wished she had some way to communicate to The ARK and him that they were okay and surviving just fine like they taught them to.

She finally let her thoughts quiet down and drifted off to sleep again with thoughts that morning would bring them sunshine and a way home.

4

Marty maneuvered the snowmobile slowly along the path, the big spotlight shining off into the woods on either side. The visibility was almost normal now that the storm had subsided.

The temperature continued to drop as the front moved into the area and if he had to guess he'd put it at -10 degrees Fahrenheit, or maybe even colder. He adjusted his face covering and felt the ice crystals that had formed on his beard and covering. He hoped Michalla and A J had found a place to build a fire and keep warm, or at least hunker down inside a snow shelter where it would hover around the freezing mark instead of -10.

So far, he'd seen no sign of them or their snowmobile, the thick layer of snow on the ground obscuring anything that would have been seen had it not snowed so hard. The light bounced off of the pristine whiteness, sometimes making his eyes water at the reflection in the crystals.

He came upon his broken-down snowmobile, the only visible color near the bottom edge. It was just a big lump in the path. He scooted around it and continued on the path toward the pasture and beyond.

As he passed the one-and-a-half-mile mark from The ARK entrance, a spot along his right side looked different than the rest of the area and he slowed to take a look. The snow was still just as thick and heavy, but the bushes looked almost trampled as if something big had run over them. Something like a snowmobile.

He shut his engine down and climbed off of the machine, hurrying to the side of the path where the bushes looked trampled. He shone his light all around and then down into the ravine that fell away just a few feet past the edge of the path. He could see nothing down there. He inspected the bushes, brushing the snow off and looking at the branches. Some were definitely broken, and those breaks looked fresh. He moved off the path to the edge of the ravine and shone the light down again. As it was panning back and forth, a reflection of something colorful made him stop. He held the light steady and realized he was looking at another snowmobile buried under the fresh snowfall.

"Michalla! A J!" His voice seemed to be swallowed up by the whiteness, and no one answered.

He stepped to the edge of the ravine, excited that he might have found them but worried that they were injured down there and not answering. He started down into the ravine, his boots slipping on the steep incline, and then his feet came out from underneath him, and he fell backward onto his rear. He slid down the ravine, gaining speed in the snow. He dropped the light and tried to slow his descent, but there was nothing to grab onto. He didn't know if he was going to fly off of some cliff, but still only thought of Michalla as he gained momentum down the side of the ravine.

As he passed the overturned snowmobile, he thought, *That's Michalla's.* And then he slammed into a tree, felt excruciating pain in his arm, and everything went black.

HARLEE STOOD JUST outside the south entrance to The ARK and looked around. It was cold. Colder than anything she'd ever been exposed to in her short life. It had to be in the negatives, and she rubbed her gloved hands together in a gesture that seemed only to make her feel better about being out here.

It was dawn. The sun was coming up over the mountains and trees, and if she weren't so worried about A J and her friends, she'd stare at the beauty of the winter scene for longer. But she had a purpose. That purpose was to find A J.

She'd stopped at Marty and Michalla's room on her way to the surface but found it empty after knocking for what seemed like thirty minutes. She had no clue as to where Marty had gone, but she figured it was outside to continue the search. She just wondered why he hadn't come to get her before leaving. They had agreed last night that they would go out together at dawn.

The fact that he hadn't come for her angered her a little, but she couldn't let those feelings cloud her judgment this morning or the resolve she had to find A J. She had to find him. He was pretty much her whole world, and though she knew she was so young to feel the way she did about him, she loved him more than she could describe. She loved him so much it hurt. And that pain was like a sore tooth at the moment. A throbbing deep inside that told her she had to do something before it was too late. He could be out there freezing to death while she was all nice and warm in the room she shared with him. Only that room had felt so lonely, and she had slept fitfully, finally getting up, her anxiety getting the best of her.

She walked over to the motor pool through the thick, new snow, and found a mechanic working on some kind of genera-tor. If she remembered correctly, his name was Roland, or Ronnie, or something like that. She stepped to him and cleared her throat. He hadn't seemed to notice her. He jumped and dropped the wrench he'd been holding. Looking up at her, his face first showed irritation, then a kind of surprise came over him, and then shyness. She almost laughed at it, but only smiled the tiniest bit. Men could be so predictable.

"Roland, right?" she asked.

"Yeah. Morning."

"Sorry to startle you. I tried to make noise."

"It's okay. Nobody is usually up this early. My shift is about to end, and I'm tired too. It's been a long, cold night."

"I bet. Hey, have you seen my friend, Marty? He was supposed to meet me so we could go out searching for the two missing members. I tried his room, but he wasn't in there."

"Yeah. I'm kinda pissed at him. He took the last snowmobile out and promised to have it back before dawn. Well, it's passed dawn. It's morning. Like breakfast time, morning. Like my shift is about over, morning. Like my ass is going to be toast for letting him take it out, morning."

She watched him fiddle with the wrench as his anxiety grew with each word, and she wondered if he was going to blow a gasket or something worse.

"That doesn't sound like Marty," she said. "When he gives his word, he always keeps it. Always."

"It doesn't appear to be the case this morning. He practically begged me to let him take it out, and I trusted him to have it back so we wouldn't get in trouble with the Colonel. Both of us."

"What time did he take it?"

"About 2:30 or so."

"He's been out there since 2:30?"

"Yep."

"I need to go find him. Can I take a snowmobile?"

"There aren't any left." He said this with a kind of anger that matched his mood. "You people keep breaking them."

"What else can I take?"

"Nothing. I'm not letting you people take any more machines out into this stuff."

"Look, I know you're upset. I can see your job is important to you. Without you, we'd be shit out of luck. I get it. But those are my friends out there. And my boyfriend. They could be dying in this cold, and I have to have a way to go look for them."

"Sorry, the only thing that's running is the 4-wheeler, and I'm not letting it out of my sight."

"What if you come with me?"

"Me?" He laughed. "I already worked the whole night shift. I'm beat. I wouldn't be worth a damn out there."

"Then you have to let me take it. Please. I promise to bring it back in one piece."

"How old are you?"

"Fifteen."

"Do you even know how to drive it?"

She felt for sure he was starting to soften. "Yes. We had three on our farm," she lied. "I ran them every day doing chores. I bet I've got more time than you on one." She smiled her brightest smile at him.

She watched him study her, the look on his face one she couldn't read. He finally huffed, turned away from her, and walked to a cabinet on the wall of the shop. He opened it and fumbled something out of it with his gloved hand. He walked back to her and handed her a set of keys.

"I'm going to regret this. Just find that Marty guy and your friends. If something happens to them, I'm sure I'll be in a crapload more trouble."

"Thanks, Roland. You won't have to worry. I'll find them."

She took the keys from him and moved to the 4-wheeler. She really had only driven it once before with A J, but she felt certain she could figure it out. She climbed up on it, put the key in the ignition, and turned it. The thing jumped forward as the starter wound up. Roland eyed her and made a face.

"Oops," she said. "It's in gear."

"You should always start vehicles with the clutch engaged."

"Right."

She squeezed the clutch and started the engine. It purred beneath her and made her feel better. She turned the front wheels and gave it a little gas, letting the clutch out slowly. The 4-wheeler began to move, and she breathed a sigh of relief as she headed out toward the path. She waved at Roland and then left him to his work.

Now, to find A J.

MICHALLA CLIMBED out of the cave and stood up in the morning light as the sun broke over the mountains. The cold made her shiver in her suit, but it was tolerable. She knew her fingers and toes would be numb soon, so she'd have to get moving to find her way to help.

A J lay inside the cave, Talia by his side and plenty of wood to keep him warm while she went for help. He told her he didn't like the idea of her out here all alone, but they really had no other choice. She was their only option for rescue, and he'd just have to suck it up and feel helpless while she trekked out of the forest and to help.

Talia came out of the cave and trotted over to her, the steam escaping from her mouth as she panted. Michalla rubbed her head.

"No, girl. You stay with A J."

"I told her to go with you!" A J's voice found her ears from inside the cave. "I'll be fine. You need her to help you find your way back."

"You sure?"

"Yes. Please be careful."

"I'll be back. With help. Come on, girl. Let's get up this ravine."

Talia wagged her tail and followed Michalla as she worked her way back to where they had left the wrecked snowmobile. It still sat inverted, buried in the snow. The only thing showing was a bit of the cowling pinstripes down near the surface. She put her hand on it as she moved past it and it shifted in the snow.

She stopped, hearing something in the distance. *Was that an engine?* She moved quickly up the ravine, trying to find footholds in the ice and snow, and used trees and rocks to help her get up. As she passed a big tree, she saw color and turned. Her breath caught in her throat.

"Marty? Marty! Oh shit!" She went to him lying crumpled and unconscious at the base of a tree and touched his face. He moaned softly but didn't move.

"Marty. Come on. Wake up. Can you hear me?"

The engine noise grew louder above her, and she looked up to the top of the ravine but could see nothing. Someone was up there on a snowmobile or something. Talia barked, and took off toward the top of the ravine.

"Go get help, girl! Go!" She cupped her hands around her mouth and shouted. "Help! We're down here! Down here!"

She wasn't sure if her voice could be heard over the sound of the engine, but she continued to shout anyway. Marty moaned again, and she knelt back down to him. She took her gloves off and touched his face. It was so cold.

"Oh no. Marty. Come on. You have to get moving!"

He moaned again, and then his eyes fluttered open. She could see him trying to focus on her. Finally, his eyes settled on hers, and he spoke.

"Hey, beautiful."

She smiled. "Damn, you scared the shit out of me."

"So did you. Where's A J?"

"He's got a broken leg. I've got him all snuggled up in a cave with a fire."

He rolled over, and then cried out. He picked up his arm to look at it. "Damn, that hurts like a mother."

She looked it over. "I don't see anything that looks weird. Still, you could have fractured it, and I can't see it."

"Feels like it's broken." He sat up.

The engine noise above them shut off, and Talia could be heard barking. Then Harlee's face appeared over the edge of the ravine.

"We're down here!" Michalla shouted, waving.

"I'm coming down!" Harlee shouted and didn't wait for an answer.

Michalla watched as she worked her way down the side of the ravine, slipping and sliding here and there, but making it without a problem.

"She did better than I did," Marty said, trying his arm again. He winced. "I don't know. It sure feels funny."

Harlee slid down to them and stood in the snow. "Where's A J?"

"He's in a cave over there," Michalla said. "He's got a broken leg. Pretty bad. He'll need help to get him up this ravine. Like a stretcher or basket kind of help. Is anybody else with you?"

"No. I'm all by myself. Nobody was awake at The ARK yet. But I'm sure we can get people here in a matter of minutes." She turned to Marty. "You didn't come get me."

"It was in the middle of the night. I couldn't sleep. I felt like I needed to be out here looking."

"It was stupid of you to go by yourself. And look, you fell, and nobody was here to help you. Stupid."

"I guess. I just didn't want to wake you."

"I was awake. Like all night."

She huffed but didn't say anything more. Michalla stood

and helped Marty up. He looked a little wobbly standing, but his arm seemed okay.

"Can you make it up the ravine?" Michalla asked.

"I think so. Shouldn't we get A J?"

"We need more help for him. He's totally incapacitated. Can't put any weight on the bad leg."

"Okay. We'll go back for help."

He started to move up the ravine and slipped. He went down hard and cried out.

"Damn. Stupid arm." He pushed himself up again and moved the arm around, trying to work it out. He started up again, and Michalla went to him and grabbed his good arm, helping him.

"I got you."

He grinned at her. "Feel like an old man."

"You're probably hypo-thermic too. You've been laying at the base of that tree for a while."

"A few hours at least. A lot of good I did you guys, huh?"

"You came for me. Nobody else did."

They climbed slowly out of the ravine and stood panting at the top on the path, Talia running around and sniffing things out. She took off after a few minutes in the direction of the south gate. Marty went to his snowmobile and cranked it up. It purred softly next to him, and Harlee climbed aboard the 4-wheeler.

A noise like the purring of a cat came to Michalla's ears, and as she looked around, it grew louder. Marty stopped what he was doing and looked up into the trees. The purring grew to a buzzing, that stuttered off and on as it grew louder. Michalla and Harlee both looked up into the tops of the trees and saw a small airplane skim the tops above them, then slam into the trees. A horrible metallic screeching sounded as the aircraft crumpled from the impact, then it tumbled out of the tops of the trees and came to a halt, nose up and upside down about twenty feet above the ground.

As they all watched in shock, the engine of the small plane burst into flame. Michalla found her feet and ran toward the crashed plane, Harlee right behind her.

Talia barked furiously up at the wreckage of the burning aircraft and Michalla strained to see inside the cockpit. It looked to contain only one person, the pilot. Harlee went to an old fallen tree next to the plane and climbed up on the stump. She reached out and grabbed the handle of the only door they could see. She yanked on it a couple of times, and it finally opened. Michalla climbed up on the fallen tree trunk too and looked inside the plane.

The man hanging upside down appeared to be out, blood running down his face and dripping onto the white snow from a cut on his chin. As she reached out to touch him, he moaned and then came awake. He blinked, shook his head, and then focused on Michalla and Harlee.

"Am I dead? Is this heaven? Angels in heaven."

"You're not dead," Michalla said. "But we have to get you out of this thing. It's on fire."

He looked up at the burning engine near his feet and frowned. "Oh damn!"

"Yeah. Can you reach your harness?"

He went to unbuckle the harness, but it wouldn't cooperate. "Too much pressure from my weight on the buckle." He began yanking at it as the fire grew bigger and now Michalla could see a real panic in his eyes. He looked at her, and she felt the panic well up in her as well.

Harlee pulled a knife from her belt and handed it to Michalla. "Here. Use this to cut him out."

She grabbed it and reached across the space to the suspended plane and worked the knife under the harness. She began sawing on the harness.

"Don't cut me," the pilot said.

"I'll try. It's that, or you burn to death."

"Okay, cut me."

She worked at the knife, sawing it back and forth as the fire crackled and burned above her head. She could smell the leaking fuel and feel the heat of the flames, and she hoped the whole thing wouldn't go up on them.

"Do you need me to come up?" Marty shouted.

"No! Be ready to try and catch him!"

The harness gave without warning, and the pilot lurched and then fell out of the door. Marty tried his best to break his fall, but he missed, and the man luckily fell into a snow bank and sank up to his hips in it. Michalla jumped down from the log just as the fuel caught fire and the flames grew bigger and more aggressive. Harlee followed, and they got the pilot up and helped drag him away from the burning wreckage. He sat panting in the snow, watching his plane burn in the trees, and then found his voice again.

"Thanks. I was a goner for sure if you folks hadn't been here." He stood slowly and looked over himself, touching the blood on his face and wiping it on his flight suit.

"It's been a while since I'd seen a plane flying around," Marty said.

"Too bad this one won't be flying again," the pilot said. "I guess the engine just decided it was done. She conked out on me, and there was nowhere to go."

"The trees seemed to cushion the crash," Michalla said.

"Didn't feel cushioned to me," he said, grinning. "I guess I'm pretty lucky."

"What's your name?" Harlee asked.

"Garrett Bourne, at your service."

"Well, Garrett. Just what the hell are you doing flying around here?" Michalla asked.

"I was heading west. California. My family is there. Or at least I think they're out there."

"Seems kind of foolish to be flying all by yourself."

"Do you see anybody else around here?"

Michalla studied him, then smiled. "Actually, there are about a hundred and fifty people not more than a mile from here."

"You're kidding."

"Nope. Want to get warm and stay for a while? You've got no transportation."

"I don't think we can just invite anyone into The ARK," Marty said. "I'm sure it will have to be cleared. What if he's carrying the virus?"

"I'm immune," Garrett said.

"That's what I thought too," Marty said. "Found out that wasn't the case."

"How are you still alive?"

"Long story."

Garrett shrugged. "I've got nowhere else to go, now. Do you think they can stitch me up?" He reached up to the wound on his face again and flinched as he touched it gingerly with his fingertips. The blood was actually starting to freeze on his face.

"Come on, pilot," Michalla said. "We'll take you back. We've got to get more help out here to get our wounded friend up out of the ravine."

"Can I be of help to your friend?"

"I don't think so. He needs a stretcher and more manpower to get him out from down there."

Michalla walked to the 4-wheeler and powered it up. She climbed on board and motioned for him to join her.

"Harlee. Ride with Marty. I'll take him in so he can get looked at."

Harlee nodded, and she followed Marty to the snowmobile, and they both climbed up.

Michalla gave the 4-wheeler some gas and felt Garrett's hand wrap around her stomach as the machine lurched.

"Hold on!"

She took off toward the south gate and home. She was anxious to get A J out of that cave and into a hospital bed. And then she would rest. She'd sleep for days.

Michalla watched as the soldiers from The ARK pulled on the rope that was attached to the sled A J lay in.

They worked him up the ravine, trying their best to make the ride as comfortable as possible for him. Talia followed next to the sled, her anxiousness clearly evident in the way she paced around A J as he was lifted up. When they got him to the top and over the lip onto the path, Michalla breathed a sigh of relief and went to him.

"Hi."

"Hey."

"Was that fun?"

"I'm not sure I'd call it fun. But it's good to be out of that cave. Thanks for getting help."

"You'd do it for me."

He grinned at her and then the soldiers were lifting him up and getting him secured to the snowmobile for the ride back to The ARK. She sat with him and held onto the sled as the snowmobile made its way down the path, the other soldiers and their vehicle following close behind. It took about twenty minutes to make it to the south entrance and then they were in the infirmary, the doctor shooing her out of the room so they could patch him up. She smiled at him as the doors closed and then she turned and felt the weariness overwhelm her.

She needed rest. Badly. She knew he was in good hands and she left him there to find her bed and sleep.

Marty was waiting for her just down the hall, his arm in a sling and his hair disheveled. He smiled at her as she came to him and fell into his good arm.

"You're a regular hero today," he said.

"I'm a beat down, tired girl, is what I am."

"You saved a downed pilot and your best friend. Not too shabby for a morning's work."

She smiled at him and kissed him on the lips. "Take me to bed."

"As you wish."

They walked hand in hand to the elevator and rode it down into the rock to the "hotel," as it was called, Marty fumbling the door open and letting her enter first. Her room looked so good. It wasn't much, but it was home, and she flopped onto the bed and sighed.

He worked her boots off, and she inched her way up to the pillows and let her head sink into the softness.

"You don't want to take your clothes off?" he asked.

"Too tired. Sleep."

He chuckled and lay down next to her. She looked into his eyes and smiled. The baby kicked softly against her belly, and she reached down and lay her fingertips on the spot. She grabbed his hand and put it there too where he could feel the little life kicking inside her.

"I'll never stop being amazed at what that feels like," he said.

"I hope it's a girl."

"I know you do. You say that all the time. If it's a boy, are you going to be able to handle it?"

She didn't answer for a few seconds, then nodded. "Of course. It's just..."

"You're afraid he'll look like him."

"Stupid. I know. I keep thinking I'm over those thoughts, but they creep back in. I guess I need to really look at how I feel about that. I mean, I'm five months pregnant. Only four more left."

"We'll be fine. You'll be fine. You'll be the best mother."

"You think?"

"I know."

She moved closer to him and let him wrap his arms around her. He winced a bit but didn't complain. She felt the world slipping away into glorious oblivion and let it happen. Sleep had never felt so good.

HARLEE MADE Talia wait outside the door, and she pushed it open to A J's room. She watched from the door as he slept, smiling and glad that he was okay, if not a little beat up. He must have sensed her because he woke and smiled at her. She came in and sat on the chair next to the bed.

"How are you feeling?" she asked.

"Good. I mean it aches a little, but it's not bad. Better than when I was out there."

"I bet. I've never broken anything. I'm sure it sucks."

"I broke my ribs. That hurt worse than this." He touched the cast on his leg, and she put her hand over his.

"I want to be the first to sign it."

"Be my guest. I don't see anyone else lining up to put a pen to it." She laughed and pulled a marker out of her pocket. "Oh. You mean right now?"

"Right now."

She leaned over and wrote something on his cast and finished with a big flourish.

"I can't read it," he said.

"You'll figure it out. Later."

She kissed him softly on the lips and spoke in a whisper, "I love you, Anderson Johns Collazo."

"Oh, God. Not the full name..."

"You love it."

"Only because it's you."

"I was so worried about you. Don't ever do anything like that again."

"Yes, ma'am. Not that I'm excited or anxious to break my leg again. I think once in a lifetime is enough."

The door creaked, and Harlee turned to see Talia's head poking in. She pushed the door the rest of the way open and trotted in, her tail wagging and her tongue hanging out. She came over, and A J rubbed her head.

"Hey, girl. Thanks for saving me. You did good."

"Do you want anything to eat?" Harlee asked. "I'm allowed to let you have anything you want."

"Anything?"

"Well, anything as long as it's beans or soup."

"I was hoping for waffles and bacon."

"You can pretend."

"I'll take some soup."

"You got it. I'll be right back."

She got up and headed for the small canteen they had on this floor, and as she rounded the corner, she bumped into the pilot they had rescued from this morning.

"Oh, hey," she said. "Did you get all stitched up?"

"Harlee, right?"

She nodded.

"Like the superhero?" he asked.

"Kinda." She studied him; his tall, well-built frame fit the green flight suit snuggly, and his blondish brown hair hung a bit long over his slate-gray eyes. The bandage on his chin hid the stitches she knew must be under it. He looked good, for just having been in a plane crash.

He sipped coffee from a paper cup, smacked his lips, and grinned. "You people got it good here. I haven't had coffee in... well...months. And it's good too."

"We have soda, too. On Wednesdays."

"Just Wednesdays?"

"Hump day."

"I bet."

She gave him a look, not quite sure what he meant. "So, are you going to stay around with us or not?"

"I haven't decided. They gave me crap when you guys brought me in. I thought at first they weren't going to help me, but they softened up when they realized I had a skill they could use. Pilot."

"I'm sure pilots are pretty scarce about now. What did you fly before?"

"F22s in the air force. Then 737s for the airlines."

"How old are you? You don't look old enough to have two careers."

"I'm old enough. Thirty-four."

"You look in your twenties."

"I guess that's a good thing. You're pretty young to be here. How did they recruit a teenager?"

"We were an experiment. Before. It's kinda a long story. I'll have to tell you another time. I'm on my way to get A J something to eat."

"Who's A J?"

"My boyfriend."

"You have a boyfriend. In this place?"

"He was part of the experiment too."

"And is he a teenager as well?"

"Yep."

"Good for you. So how old is Michalla?"

"I'll let her tell you. If she wants to."

"Right."

She smiled at him. "You got the hots for her?"

He tilted his head a little and studied her for a second. "Just curious to know a little about the angels who rescued me." He grinned at her.

"Angels, huh? I've never been anybody's angel. I'm sure Michalla hasn't either."

"That's what popped into my head when I saw your beautiful faces in front of me hanging upside down strapped into the plane. The plane I should have died in. Thanks, by the way. If I didn't tell you before."

"You did."

He sipped from his coffee again, the silence between them now growing uncomfortable. She finally broke it.

"I gotta go. A J's starving and I promised him I'd be right back."

"Sure. I'm gonna look around. See what there is to see in this place. Do you know where Michalla is? I kind of wanted to thank her."

"She's probably in her room."

"Where is that, exactly..."

She hesitated, not sure if this stranger was all right yet. He seemed nice enough. Oh, what the heck. Michalla would probably be upset if she scared him off.

"She's in room B23. In the lower levels. Take the elevator all the way down. That's where the living quarters are."

"Thanks. I'll go and find her."

"Good. Okay, I'll talk to you later."

"Later."

He moved away, and she watched him turn the corner. She

shook her head to herself and then headed for the canteen and A J's soup.

MARTY WATCHED MICHALLA SLEEP, his aching arm keeping him from sleeping himself. If he wanted, he could have gotten some painkillers and been sacked out like her, but he didn't like how they made him feel. The loss of control was something he avoided at all costs. Not that he had anything to worry about down here in the bowels of The ARK, but it was just the way he felt.

He shifted, trying to get his arm in a better place and she stirred, rolling over and moving away from him. He felt a pang of loss for just a second, and then realized he was being stupid. She was right here, right next to him. In the place that felt most comfortable to him. Her soft blonde hair covered the side of her face, and he reached up to brush it away and stopped. Let her rest. He could see her any time he wanted.

A knock at the door made him flinch, and she stirred again but didn't wake. He got up quietly and went to the door. He expected it to be Harlee, so when he found himself face to face with the pilot from this morning, he could feel his eyes widen in surprise.

"Oh. Hey," Garrett said. "I thought this was Michalla's room." He took a step back, looked at the room number on the wall, and then in both directions. "I could have sworn Harlee said B23."

"This is her room. She's sleeping." Marty eyed him and wondered what he was doing here. Why wasn't he being watched or interrogated or investigated or something official? He couldn't believe that as rigid as the military was about this facility, he could just be wandering around after only a few hours. Was he something more than Marty or Michalla thought?

"She's here, then."

"Yeah. Like I said, she's sleeping. She needs the rest. She was out in that mess of a storm all night and all day yesterday."

"Right. My bad. I didn't realize she had stayed up all night."

Marty watched as the pilot seemed to study him, then looked around him into the room. What? Did the guy not believe that she was asleep? Out in the woods after the crash, Marty had felt good about the guy. That maybe he was all right, just had a bad day. But now, he was picking up a vibe from him he didn't like. Not one bit.

"Was there something you wanted with her?"

"If she's asleep, how come you're here?"

"This is my room."

"I thought it was her room."

"It is her room."

"So, it's both of your rooms?"

Marty nodded.

"Is there a shortage of space or something? Do all of you share rooms?"

"No. No shortage. We asked to share a room."

The pilot—Garrett was his name if Marty remembered correctly—shifted his feet and made a face. "You two are together then."

"Yeah. We're together. Can you hold it down a bit? I don't want to wake her. She's pretty wiped."

"Sorry. I'll leave you two alone. I just came by to thank her. For saving my life out there. I should be dead."

"I'll let her know. I'm sure she'll appreciate you coming by."

Marty started to close the door, and Garrett put his hand on it, stopping it. Marty looked up, expectantly.

"What was your name again?" he asked.

"Marty."

"Right. Okay, Marty. Good talking to you. I'll see you around."

"Yep. See you around."

He closed the door, and Garrett didn't stop him this time. He stared at the wood of the closed door for a second, his brain spinning a mile a minute; the vibe from the encounter definitely a bit confrontational. Maybe he needed to rethink his opinion of the pilot. If he were to guess, the man was attracted to Michalla and had been surprised that she and Marty were an item. A small pang of jealousy edged into his thoughts, and he didn't like the feeling. Michalla's voice brought him out of it.

"Was someone here?"

He turned to her in the bed. "The pilot guy. Garrett. He was looking for you."

"What did he want?"

"To thank you for saving his life. At least that's what he said."

"Oh. That was nice of him. I'll talk to him later."

She shifted again, and as Marty lay back down, her eyes closed again. Just that quickly. He touched her face, and she reached up to clasp his hand in hers, smiling.

"Hold me," she whispered.

"As you wish."

He pulled her tighter to him, and she snuggled inside his arms. She was snoring softly in a matter of minutes. He closed his eyes, putting thoughts of Garrett and her out of his head, and fell asleep himself before he even realized what had happened.

6

Michalla woke and found herself alone.

The space next to her felt cold, and she wondered how long Marty had been gone. There was no clock in the room or watch on her wrist, so she had no idea what time it was. It felt like days had passed, but of course, she had no idea how long she'd been asleep. She sat up and rubbed her face. Her body ached from what seemed like head to toe, and she stretched in front of her bed trying to loosen herself up. She made her way to the small bathroom that made up the other room in the space and relieved herself. The door opened, and Marty walked in.

"Oh good, you're up," Marty said.

She went to him and let him pull her tightly to him. "Damn," she said. "You feel so good."

"You scared the crap out of me."

"You didn't do too bad a job of that yourself. How's your arm?"

"Fine."

She gave him a look.

"Okay, it's sore as hell, but at least it's not broken. I'll be good in no time."

"I want to see A J."

"He's still in the infirmary. I'm sure they'll let you visit."

"Oh, they'll let me. Go with me."

"Sure. Do you want to eat first? I mean it's almost dinner time."

She blanched. "Like, dinner time the next day?"

"Yep."

"I've been asleep this whole time."

"Unless you've been doing stuff in here I'm not aware of."

She shook her head. "I guess I was completely wiped out. A J probably thinks I've abandoned him."

"I doubt it. You saved him, remember?"

"I only did what I had to do so we'd survive."

"That's called saving him. You did better than I did. You had to save me too."

She pulled away from him. "I'll eat after I see him. I'm feeling pretty guilty for staying away this long."

"Up to you. They're having venison stew."

It was her favorite, but she needed to see A J first. "A J. Then stew. Come on."

She pushed past him, and he followed her out the door closing up their little room behind him. She led the way down the dim corridor, the only lights a few bare bulbs spaced far apart, the soft glow of the incandescents eerie if she thought too hard about it. At the elevator, she tapped her foot impatiently as they waited.

"You needed the rest," Marty said.

"I know. Still, I feel guilty."

"A J will never feel the way you think he will. He adores you. Worships the ground you walk on. You're like his queen or something."

"Or something."

She knew A J cared about her, but the way Marty talked he

was in love with her or something. She loved him herself, but in a way that was more sisterly, or even motherly, if she thought too long about it. She rubbed her belly absently as more motherly instincts kicked in. Marty came up to her and put his hand over her's on her belly.

"Is he practicing his soccer kicks?"

"She's practicing her Judo."

He grinned at her. "Okay, I'll give you that."

The elevator arrived, and they slipped in, riding it up to the top floors where the infirmary was shoved into a space between the motor pool entrance and the cafeteria. It seemed like the person who designed the facility had forgotten to add it, and plopped it in any spare space he or she could find before their mistake had been noticed. Or maybe after their mistake had been noticed.

They walked down the hallway and as she turned the corner, she almost ran into the pilot she'd help rescue. Garrett, if she remembered correctly.

"Whoa!" he said, stepping back and keeping his cup of coffee balanced in his hand. "Hey. I was wondering when I'd see you again. Thought you fell off the face of the earth or something."

"I was resting up."

She turned to see Marty eyeing the man. Something passed between him and Garrett in an instant and if she had to guess it wasn't complimentary.

"You probably needed it."

"Do you remember Marty?"

"Sure. Good to see you again." He stuck his hand out, and Marty shook it but said nothing. Garrett turned back to Michalla. "I never got to thank you properly for saving my ass. I'd be cooked bacon if not for you and your friend, Harlee. I already thanked her, but I wanted to make sure you knew how much I appreciated you risking it all for little ole me."

"It was nothing."

"It was everything. Like I said, I'd be toast if not for you."

"What happened anyway? Why did the plane come down?"

"Engine. Decided it didn't want to live anymore, I guess. I'd put a bunch of hours on it since everything went to crap and with nobody to do maintenance, it felt the need to let me down. Don't blame her. If I knew anything about taking care of that engine, she'd probably still be flying."

"Where were you headed? Not much up here anymore."

"Trading post. Just on the other side of the hills. I do some business with the survivors there. Barter and stuff like that. Then west. To family."

"What are you going to do now?"

"Don't know. They say I can stay on a bit longer if I like. I'm trying to decide if I like it here. Maybe if I had a reason to stay. You know, somebody to make it worthwhile." He grinned.

She studied him for a few seconds, not quite sure she had heard him correctly. Was he really hitting on her right there in front of Marty? She make a kind of laughing cough in her throat and glanced at Marty who now scowled next to her.

"Not too many left here that aren't already taken, my friend," Marty said, wrapping his arm around Michalla.

Garrett watched them with a small smile on his lips and nodded slowly.

"Right. I was getting that impression. I guess I'll make up my mind soon enough."

"Well, we're on our way to see A J," Michalla said.

"The kid who drove you two off a cliff?" Garrett asked.

"He didn't drive us off a cliff. It was a whiteout."

"Sure. If you say so."

She scowled at him. *Pompous asshole*, she thought to herself. She was beginning to regret having saved him. He looked to be more trouble than she originally thought. Still, there was something about him…

"We'll talk to you later," she finally said and moved around him. He watched them walk past.

"Definitely."

Marty pulled her closer to him as they walked away and when they were out of earshot he said, "Can you believe that guy? What a dork."

"He doesn't seem to have a confidence problem."

"Pilots. They're all hotshots."

She grinned up at him. "I thought you wanted to be a pilot once?"

"Maybe not so much now."

She bumped her hip into his and continued to smile at him. "I do believe you're jealous, Mr. Marty."

"Of him? Hell no. He's not your type."

"You're right about that."

He finally grinned. "Okay, maybe a little."

"Good. Keeps you in your place."

"Yes, ma'am."

They reached the infirmary and found A J's room. She knocked, then pushed it open without waiting for a response. She walked in on the nurse giving A J a sponge bath. Michalla stood there in the doorway as he tried his best to cover up.

"You could knock," A J said, his face turning red.

"I did," Michalla said, grinning. "I've seen you naked before, anyway."

"When?"

"In Florida. A couple of times. Remember? Swimming in those springs and that river."

"Oh, right. Still..."

"Do you want me to wait outside?"

He looked at the nurse who picked up her little basin. "I'm done anyway," the nurse said. "You can visit with him." She smiled and left the room.

Michalla went to him, kissed him on the forehead, and put

her hand to his face. "You look pretty good."

"I feel like crap. My leg itches like crazy in this thing."

He grabbed up a pen and poked it under the cast, scratching as best he could.

"How long do you have to keep it?" she asked.

"A month, the Doc said. Stupid."

"That's not too bad. I would have thought it would be longer."

"I still can't believe I drove us off the edge. I feel like an idiot."

"I would have done the same thing. It was impossible to see out there."

"I guess."

"Where's Harlee?" she asked.

"She went to grab something to eat while they bathed me. She's due back any minute."

Harlee appeared on cue, pushing the door open and carrying in a bag of something that smelled pretty good. Michalla guessed it to be the venison stew that Marty had talked about. She realized how hungry she was.

"Hey," Harlee said. "I was wondering if you were ever going to wake up."

"I was exhausted, apparently," Michalla said.

"She slept like a log," Marty said. "Every time I went in to check on her she was snoring up a storm."

"I don't snore."

Marty raised an eyebrow. Michalla huffed but said nothing more.

Harlee set the bag on the tray next to A J and started to unpack it. "You're hungry, right?" she asked him.

"Starved," he said. "Smells fantastic."

"It was pretty good. I had some while you had your bath." She grinned at him. "How was that, by the way? Getting washed by a pretty nurse."

"Embarrassing as hell."

"You probably loved it. I bet you got all excited." Her eyes flashed, and he turned red again.

Marty laughed. "I would have. She was pretty cute."

"Hey," Michalla said. "I'm right here."

"I was not excited," A J said. "In any way. It was the worst."

Harlee bent over and kissed him on the lips. "I should have stayed to watch."

"Harlee..."

She continued to grin as she took the cup of stew out of the bag and set a plastic spoon down next to it on his tray. "Should I feed you?"

"I can manage just fine, thank you."

Michalla smiled at the two of them as they played like an old married couple. A J was pretty cute in his angst, and Harlee really cared for him. It showed in her eyes and the way she wanted to take care of him. They were too damn young to be so close, but there was no denying their love for each other. And for that, Michalla was glad. She glanced at Marty who must have been thinking the same thing because he smiled back at her and looked embarrassed.

"That pilot guy's been looking for you," Harlee said. "He's kinda pushy. Cute, but pushy."

"He found me," Michalla said, but added nothing else. Harlee eyed her but didn't ask any more questions.

"Where's Talia?" Michalla asked, and the dog stuck her head out from under the bed at the sound of her name. "There you are. Come here, girl."

Talia crawled out and came to Michalla, her tail wagging furiously.

"Such a good girl. I'm so proud of you. Without your help, we'd probably have died out there." She rubbed the big dog's head and sides and smiled at her.

A J took the lid off of the stew, and the smell filled the room. Michalla's mouth started to water. "That smells so good."

"It is pretty good," A J said with a mouthful as he chewed.

"If you want any, you'd better hurry," Harlee said. "They were almost out."

Michalla looked at A J who waved his hand. "I'm fine. I'm glad you came to see me, but if you've been sleeping as long as Marty says, you're probably starving. Go. Harlee's here to keep me company."

"You sure? I feel bad that I slept while you suffered. You probably needed me, and I wasn't here."

"What? To hold my hand?" She smiled at him, and he shook his head. "I'm a big boy."

"You are. My brave, big boy." She went to him and kissed him on the forehead again. He turned red.

"Sheesh."

Her smile grew even bigger as Harlee smiled back at her and then laughed.

She went to Marty who put his arm around her and then she tugged on his shirt. "Come on. Feed me."

"Yes, Ma'am."

Michalla left A J to his stew and Harlee and felt a little pang of guilt at leaving him again so soon. But her stomach growled loudly in the hall, and she let her hunger lead her away. For now.

HARLEE CLOSED the door softly to A J's room, not wanting to wake him, and slipped quietly down the hall toward the elevator. The nurse had let her stay as long as she wanted, and now that it was late, the facility was dark and quiet at night. She wondered what time it was and as she reached the elevator, she looked up at the lone clock on the wall.

12:30 a.m.

Damn. She'd probably overstayed her welcome, and she yawned at how tired she was. Even though all she'd done is sit with him and help him here and there, the fact that he was hurt and in pain seemed to sap her energy. Who knew how tiring worrying about somebody you loved could be?

She smiled at the thought of loving a boy she'd only met a few months ago. Before the Pukes, she'd never even considered that she had the capacity to care for someone so much. All she had worried about was her friends in school, whether her mom would know about the weed she'd kept hidden under her mattress, and whether or not her pics and videos she'd posted to social media were getting the 'likes' she felt they deserved. She shook her head. Such a waste. Looking back on how things had been she could see how clearly what she had thought so important in her life looked foolish and meaningless now. She pressed the button for the elevator as a pang of loss for her sister shot through her memory. The both of them had spent so much time taking pictures and movies of each other. It seemed their only connection, and now she wished they had found other ways to make their lives more meaningful.

She was so lost in the memory of her sister that when the elevator door opened, and she took a step toward it as she looked up, the scene that spread out before brought a scream to her lips.

A body lay crumpled on the floor of the elevator, one arm lying in a pool of bright red blood and the other bent at a funny angle near the bloody face of the nightshift mechanic, Roland. His mouth lay open in a silent scream as his lifeless eyes stared up at the ceiling. His legs lay curled up underneath his body. When she got control of herself, she stepped to Roland and felt for a pulse at his wrist.

Nothing.

Footsteps raced down the hall toward her, and Sergeant

Hector Wilton ran up and looked into the car and her.

"Oh, damn," he said, pulling his firearm from its holster and looking into her eyes. "Is that Roland?"

She nodded, her lip starting to quiver as tears fought to show themselves.

"What happened?" The Sergeant looked at her with accusatory eyes, the pistol held in both his hands pointing at the floor.

"I don't know," Harlee said. "The elevator opened, and I found him like this."

Hector looked around, his body tense and at the ready, and when he realized it was just the two of them, he holstered the gun and reached out his hand toward her.

"Come on. Get out of there."

She took his hand and let him lead her out of the elevator. The doors started to close, and he stepped to them and held them open with his foot. He pulled a pocket knife from a sheath on his belt and wedged the blade between the door and the track, preventing it from closing.

"You okay?" he finally asked.

She nodded, then shook her head, no. "He's dead," she said. "Who could have done this?"

"I don't know, but I'm going to find out. I've got to go to the phone on the wall over there. Why don't you wait over by the stairs. You know. So you don't have to look at him while I call this in."

She nodded and moved toward the stairs as she watched him go to the phone and dial a number from memory. She looked toward the elevator and could still see one booted foot lying at a weird angle against the wall of the elevator car. A small splash of blood had spattered the wood-grained wall above it. She shuddered and then her legs kind of gave out, and she slid down the wall to the floor where she put her head down to her knees and started to cry.

PART II

Dak

&

Cori

7

_____

C ori rested her hand softly on her belly and smiled to
herself.

The life growing inside of her was too small for
her to feel any movement, but she still liked to think her baby
could feel its mother's warmth passing through the layers of
cloth and skin and muscle. A hand reached over from her right
and gripped hers in its fingers. She looked up into Dak's eyes as
he smiled at her. She turned her hand over and let her fingers
intertwine with his, the strength in his grip something she
cherished from the first time she held his hand all those
months ago.

A little turbulence jolted them in their seats as they cruised
in the TBM850 at ten thousand feet and then the small plane
settled into the steady hum she'd been lulled by for the last
hour. Her dad, Noah Dresdon, sat in the right seat as co-pilot,
the left seat occupied by Flynn McPhee. She watched as Flynn
flipped some switch on the instrument panel and a little green
light lit up. He seemed satisfied with it and switched it back off.
Chet Hopkins, sat in the seat directly in front of Cori, his head

hanging down to his chest as he dozed. The man was still a mystery to her, but he seemed to respect and admire her father, so that made him all right in her book. The rest of their small band of survivors had stayed behind at the Cape, watching over the younger ones and maintaining a presence on the base so as to discourage others from settling into the facility.

They were heading north, as far as the fuel in the little plane would take them, and then they would be on foot or if they were lucky, some other form of transportation. Flynn would drop them off and then fly back to the Cape to take care of his daughter, Terrina. As a diabetic, she needed his care, and though he felt obligated to act as pilot, he would never consider leaving her for more than a day at most. Noah and Flynn had argued briefly over whether or not Flynn should ferry them, but when it came down to it, the small plane was just too valuable to leave at some small airfield, waiting for them to return to it. Flynn would ferry it back to the base where it would be safe, and Cori, Dak, Noah, and Chet would have to manage to get home on their own once they'd found Michalla.

And that was really what it was all about. Finding Michalla and getting their family back together. Cori was so excited she could barely sit still, but she knew they still had a tough journey ahead. Not only were they heading up north based on hearsay from Flynn, but they didn't even know if they would be able to get onto the base where they suspected she was. Or if she'd be free to leave with them. For all Cori knew, her sister was some kind of prisoner being held by the only acting government that still existed within the conterminous United States of America.

"You got serious all of a sudden," Dak said into her ear. "Worried?"

"I was just thinking of Michalla. I'm excited. And scared. What if we can't find her? What if they won't let her go? What if...?"

Dak squeezed her fingers. "We'll find her. I know it. And you guys will be together again."

Cori smiled and looked down at her hand in his. "I can't wait to tell her I'm pregnant. Of everyone I know, she'll be the most excited for me."

"Hey, I'm the most excited."

She looked up into his eyes, the smile growing on her face. "I know. You know what I mean."

"I do. From what you've said of her, you two have a bond that nothing can separate. I can't wait to meet her."

"She's a twin of me. People always thought we were real twins. We just look so much alike."

Dak sat back in his seat, and Cori looked out the window at the world rushing by below them. The tiny trees and roads and abandoned cars all slipped beneath her as they moved further north. She felt a flutter in her belly and took in a quick breath. She turned to Dak with an astonished look on her face.

"It moved! I felt it."

"Are you sure? It's kind of early don't you think?"

"It was like a little flutter inside. Just a faint feeling of movement."

"It was gas."

She whacked him on the arm, laughing. "No, it wasn't. I don't have gas."

"You could have fooled me. I sleep with you, remember."

She whacked him again.

A noise filled the cabin as some kind of alarm sounded from the front of the plane. She turned and watched as her dad leaned forward and flipped some switches. The plane slowed dramatically, the tension in her seatbelt giving the sensation of momentum. She turned to Dak whose look of concern was not lost on her. Then the turbine engine sputtered and stopped.

"Complete electrical failure!" Flynn said.

"I'm feathering the prop," Noah said, as he moved a lever

and the propeller in front of the plane slowed and then stopped.

To Cori, it was surreal. The propeller was supposed to be spinning. Not just sitting there doing nothing. The sound of the air rushing across the airframe was the only sound that could be heard and the quiet, along with the stillness of the prop caused panic to well up inside her. She gripped Dak's hand tightly and watched as Chet sat up in front of her.

"What's going on?" Chet asked, but nobody in the cockpit answered as she watched her dad and Flynn work the controls and all the dials and switches. Her dad reached up and flipped some breakers and then flipped them back.

"Try it now," he said.

Flynn flipped some switches of his own and nothing happened.

"Nothing. Prepare for a dead-stick landing."

"Shit."

"Dad? What's happening?"

"Not now, honey. I'm kinda busy. Make sure you're buckled in tight."

Cori checked her seat belt and watched Dak do the same. The expression on his face was something she wished she could manage. He looked calm. Serious, but calm. He smiled at her.

"It's gonna be all right," he said. "Your dad and Flynn are the best. Hell, your dad went to space. He can handle this."

Cori turned back to the front and watched as her dad flipped through some kind of manual checklist as Flynn worked the controls.

"What have we got that's close?" Flynn asked.

"One here, and one here. This one is kind of small, but it's closer."

"We've got a short distance of glide on this airframe. We're already down under 8000. I think we have to go for the smaller one."

"It's right at the limit," Noah said.

"We have no other choice. Unless we put it down on a road or in a field."

Noah looked out the window. "Big highway to the right. But it looks congested with abandoned cars."

"Right. I'm heading for that small airfield. It's grass and will probably handle the belly landing better."

"I can try and pump the gear down."

"No. I don't want to risk getting it halfway down and having to land with things sticking out of the bottom that will only hurt us. We belly it in."

Noah nodded. He turned to the back and spoke to Cori, Dak, and Chet. "We're going to have to try and make it to a small airport up ahead and put it down on the grass without landing gear. It will be rough and bumpy, but we should be fine. As soon as the plane stops, Dak, you open the door and get everyone clear of the plane. It probably won't catch fire on a grass surface, but it could. Our tanks are still pretty full."

"Dad?"

"Yes, honey?"

"Are we gonna be okay?"

"We are. Flynn's the best. When I say, put your head down to your knees and your arms over your head. Okay?"

She nodded. He stared at her for a second more and then turned back to face forward. The wind rushing past the airframe was the only sound now, and she looked out the small window as the trees and roads and houses grew closer. They were descending pretty fast, and she only hoped they would make it to the airport. If they hit trees or something else they might not survive.

A little turbulence jolted the small plane, and she felt her stomach do a flip. She put her hand to her belly and felt a tear track down her face. The thought of her baby growing inside her made her worry even more. What if the crash injured her or the baby? She pushed the thought from her head and felt Dak grab her hand and hold it. It was warm and dry, and he looked calm, though she knew he must be feeling something more than that. She saw Chet turn and glance at the two of them, the fear in his eyes clearly evident, but he seemed to take a deep breath and find a way to calm himself. He turned back to face the front. Out the front of the windshield, all Cori could see was blue sky. Pretty blue sky.

"It's gonna be close," Flynn said. He fought the controls a bit and then she saw him flinch as a scraping sound came from beneath her feet. She watched as a few tree branches flew up around them and then it grew quiet again.

"Brace for landing!" Noah yelled.

Cori put her head down and her arms over her head and waited. It seemed like they floated forever, the gentle up and down of the plane as it settled in silence something that didn't seem right. Then, a violent shudder and deceleration as a horrible scraping and screeching filled the plane's compartment. The plane shook violently as she turned her head to look toward Dak, but his head was down and covered by his arms. The shaking and rattling seemed to go on forever but never worsened. Then she could feel the plane slow and finally stop as silence settled into the cabin.

"Everybody out!" Noah shouted.

Dak unbuckled his seat belt and helped her with hers and then went to the door where he worked the controls. It swung up and open, and he let Cori go out first into the bright sunlight. She ran from the plane, feeling Dak right behind her. She stumbled, the adrenaline coursing through her veins betraying her. She went to her knees and then felt strong hands around her lifting her up. She got her feet under her again and ran with Dak until it felt safe. They stopped and turned to see.

Chet ran up right next to them as her dad and Flynn exited the plane. Flynn had blood running down his face and looked dazed. Her dad turned back and helped him away from the plane. A few small tendrils of smoke drifted up from the bottom of the plane, but it didn't catch fire and after a moment the smoke dissipated, and the sounds of the surrounding environment slowly returned. Birds sang in the trees and insects made their sounds in the high grass. Cori shivered at the cool air and wrapped her bare arms around herself. She was still wearing shorts and no sleeves for the temps in Florida, but she had packed colder weather gear in her backpack. It was still on the plane, and she hoped it didn't catch fire.

Noah came up with Flynn holding his head, and she went to him.

"Let me look," she said.

Flynn knelt in the grass, and she probed just under his hairline with gentle fingers. He had a good-sized gash that was deep and all the way to the bone. It was bleeding like crazy. She tore some cloth from her shirt and pressed it to the wound.

"Hold this on it with some pressure. You're going to need some sutures. I have some of those special bandages with built-in closure pulls in my backpack. I'll get you fixed up in a bit."

"Don't go back to the aircraft just yet," Flynn said. "It could still catch fire."

"Okay."

"Is everybody okay?" Noah asked.

"I'm a little shaken, but not physically hurt," Cori said.

"I'm fine," Dak said.

"I crapped myself," Chet said, and then grinned. "Nice job with the landing you two. We're alive, and that's all that matters."

"Not all," Flynn said. "We no longer have a plane. How am I going to get back to Terrina?"

"We'll figure it out," Noah said, kneeling in the grass, the adrenaline rush of the landing finally hitting him as his body tried to calm itself. "There might be another aircraft at this airport."

He looked around, and Cori followed his gaze. It was more of an airstrip than an airport. The runway was grass that was overgrown into weeds that grew to about thigh height. Three lone hangars stood about 500 yards away next to each other, one door of the middle hangar hanging canted and broken. She could see nothing inside the structure. Surrounding the small airstrip, thick woods led off in all directions, the leaves changing colors with the fall season and a cold wind blowing in from what looked to be the north.

"Where are we, Dad?"

"Somewhere in Kentucky. The last I saw on the GPS in the cockpit before the electrical system failed showed us near a town called Calhoun."

Cori's heart sank. They weren't even halfway to where they needed to be. Michalla was a long way off, and that meant they would have to travel even farther on foot or in some other form of transportation. No cars could be seen, but there was a lone beat-up truck parked next to the last hangar. It sat in the over-grown weeds and looked abandoned long ago. If she were to guess, she was sure it wouldn't start.

"I think it's safe to get the things from the cargo hold," Noah said. "Dak, Chet. You want to help me?"

Dak nodded, and Chet turned to follow Noah. Cori stayed with Flynn who had turned a distinct shade of white as he sat in the grass.

"I don't feel good," he said.

"You're going into shock. It's normal with this kind of injury."

"I feel like I'm going to throw up."

"Just let it happen if it does."

He looked at her, his expression unreadable, then he turned and vomited in the grass. She held him as he retched for a few minutes and then he sat back up.

"Better?" she asked.

He nodded. "Sorry."

"It's okay," she smiled. "I've had to deal with worse in the hospital. Let's look at that wound."

She reached up and lifted his hand away. The blood flowed immediately, and she pressed it back down.

"You've got a real good bleeder there," she said. "We might have to cauterize it."

"Like with heat?"

She nodded.

"Great. I'm sure that will feel good."

"It will hurt like a mother."

"Thanks."

But he grinned at her.

The men walked up carrying all the backpacks and dropped them in the grass. Dak held his M4 in his hand and checked it over. He leaned it up against his backpack and picked up Cori's checking it over as well. He seemed satisfied that the weapons had survived the crash without damage.

"Dad, we need to build a fire pretty quick. I've got to cauterize Flynn's wound and get it bandaged up." Cori stood and looked at the forest that surrounded them, then back to the three buildings. "Do you think we should take shelter in one of those hangars?"

"Flynn, can you walk to the buildings over there?" Noah asked.

"Yeah. I'm fine, just a little shaky."

He wobbled a little bit as he stood. Cori reached out and

steadied him. "Maybe you better lean on me or one of the guys as we make our way over there."

"Right."

Dak came over, and Flynn put his arm around him, Cori grabbing up her backpack and Flynn's along with it. Chet picked up Dak's and his own and Noah carried the weapons. They trekked across the overgrown runway toward the hangars, leaving a little wake behind them in the tall grass. Something skittered away in front of them, and Cori wondered how long before the runway wasn't recognizable as something man-made. She figured another six months.

The trees ringing the strip were beautiful in their fall colors, the oranges, reds, and golds of the leaves shimmering in the breeze that blew across the open area. Cori shivered a bit from the cool air and couldn't wait to change into something that fit the weather a bit better. Or at least stand in front of a warm fire.

Three big bangs sounded in a row, and they froze.

"Gunshots," Dak said. "From the north."

"Looks like we're not alone. From the air, we could see a small town to the north. Just a brief glimpse of it before all the action happened." Noah pointed in the direction of north, and they all listened for a minute or so longer. No other shots sounded.

Noah led the way toward the buildings, and as they approached the middle one with the broken door, Cori could see that all three were not in the best of shape. If she were to guess, they were probably constructed over fifty years ago or more. The roofs sagged on all three and the paint had peeled and chipped, as if the lack of attention from their owners was something they were used to. Noah held his rifle at the ready as he approached the opening. He looked inside, then stepped over the canted door and disappeared. They waited for a minute or so, and then he reappeared again.

"It's clear. Come on in and get out of the wind."

Cori followed Dak and Flynn into the hangar, and when her eyes adjusted, she could see an old Piper Cub sitting rotting at the center of the building. Its yellow paint faded and worn, bits of the wing covering hung in tatters from the skeletal frame beneath it. The place smelled of oil and grease, the dirt floor dark black from some long-ago treatment to keep it clear. She wondered if they started a fire in here if the whole place would go up. At the back right side, a small room sat with one window and one door. Noah went to it, pushed the door open, and stepped inside. He came back out after a minute.

"Just a desk and chair and some old parts on a shelf. This place has probably been long abandoned since even before The Pukes."

"Looks like it's home for a bit," Cori said. "We need some firewood."

"I'll go and find some," Dak said. "Be back in a bit."

He disappeared out through the broken door, and Cori busied herself going through her backpack and the first aid kit she had in there finding what she needed to get Flynn fixed up. Dak returned a few minutes later with an armful of sticks and wood, and he dropped everything near the door for ventilation. He got the fire going in no time, and Cori went to it, the warmth something that felt good on her skin. She put the blade of her knife into the coals and let it get red hot. When she pulled it out, it glowed in the low light. She went to Flynn.

He eyed her but said nothing.

"You know what's going to happen," Cori said. "Do you want something to bite down on?"

He shook his head rapidly. "Just get it over with."

She moved his hand away from the wound, the blood still flowing freely without the pressure on it. She glanced at his face and saw that his eyes were shut. She pressed the glowing tip of the knife blade to the wound and heard it sizzle. Flynn flinched but didn't make a sound. She worked the blade along the gash, the smell of burning hair mixing with the smoke from the fire. She pulled the knife away, and the bleeding had just about stopped. A little oozing of blood was all that came from the gash. Flynn let the breath he'd been holding out and opened his eyes.

"All done," she said, smiling. "Now let's get that special bandage on it."

She prepared the suture-like bandage and shaved a bit of the hair from his scalp with a cool knife she got from Dak. She applied some disinfectant from the first aid kit and then the bandage over the gash and pulled the little tabs to close the wound. It worked like a charm, and she smiled.

"These things were pretty new before the Pukes. I'd only seen them used once or twice. They work really well."

"It stings like a mother," Flynn said.

"I have some pain pills. Do you want one?"

"No. I need to keep my wits about me. I'll be all right."

"Any dizziness, headache, nausea?"

"Yes."

"Which?"

"All of them."

She smiled as she put a bigger gauze bandage over the special sutures and secured it with some tape. It would pull out hair when it was removed, but it was the best she could do. She sat back on her heels and inspected her work.

"I'll think you'll live."

"Thank you."

"My pleasure."

He stood, looking much better than before, and went to his own backpack where he fished out a long-sleeved shirt and slipped it on. She shivered and decided she better change into something warmer. As the sun went down, it would get pretty chilly tonight.

She rummaged through her things and found jeans and a

pullover hoody. She went into the little office and changed in some privacy. After, she looked at the desk and went to it. She pulled open the drawers but found nothing of real value she could use. It was mostly just broken pencils and a few paper clips. There was a picture of the Piper Cub back in its glory days, a smiling man standing next to the wing with his hand resting on a strut. She had been beautiful at some point, and it made Cori sad to know that she would probably never fly again.

Cori moved back into the bigger space and stood next to the fire, warming herself. Dak rested up against his backpack, Skitch at his feet, the German Shepherd watching her with eyes that held interest and wonder. She went to him and rubbed his head between his ears. His tail wagged and thumped against the black dirt floor.

"You look just fine, boy," she said. "Did Dak check you over?"

"He's fine," Dak said.

"Did you check him over?"

"Yes. He's fine."

She smiled at Dak and rubbed Skitch's sides. She sat next to Dak against his backpack and leaned her head on his shoulder.

"I'm suddenly very tired."

"It's the stress of the crash landing. And you had to burn a man on purpose with a hot, glowing knife."

"There was that."

"How are you feeling?"

"You mean...you know?"

He nodded.

She touched her belly. "I think everything is good. I don't feel any different. The landing was bumpy but not especially violent. I think she's good."

"You mean, he."

"We'll see."

She liked the banter between them. To her, it meant he cared about their unborn child. That he just might make a good father. Even in a world where there wasn't much left to be grateful for, they would both find happiness in a new life.

Of that, she was sure.

8

Cori opened her eyes, and the dark silhouette of a man framed in the door took shape in her vision. She was in that state of half-wakefulness, between the dream she had been having of her past life and the reality of her present one. She closed her eyes again for a few seconds and then they flew open as she came fully awake.

The door was empty.

No man. No silhouette. Not even a sound. She sat up and looked around the hangar. Everybody else was asleep, the fire smoking in the middle of the circle of sleeping bags and blankets. Dak faced away from her at her feet, and even Skitch snored softly at his head. She must have been dreaming.

She sighed, laid back down, and stared up at the roof of the building. A noise came from outside, and she sat up again. The scrape of a shoe on the gravel came to her ears, and she reached for her rifle. Skitch came awake and looked to the door. A low growl came from his throat. She stood, and crept to the opening, the rifle held at the ready. She felt Skitch rub against her leg and felt a little better.

She looked out of the door into the morning mist and saw

nothing in the open field where the runway sat. She looked right, and then left, and for a second wasn't sure what she was looking at. Then the man who was crouched a few feet away stood up fully and held his rifle out at the end of his arm, signaling his surrender. She pointed her M4 at him and stepped completely outside. Skitch growled but stayed next to her. The man's eyes focused on the dog. He looked afraid.

"I don't mean you no harm, lady," he said, his deep voice carrying a southern drawl with it, a kind of sing-song way of speaking that if she wasn't so tense, she might find soothing.

"What are you doing here?"

"I saw the plane," he pointed out toward the TBM, "and I saw the smoke coming from your fire. I was just curious who was here and if they were all right."

"Lower that gun to the ground. Slowly."

He did as he was told and then stood up straight again. He was a massive man. Easily six foot five if not more. He was thick about the shoulders, and his arms looked as if he could pick up a car engine all by himself. His long beard hung to his chest, and bits of food, or twigs could be seen. His blue eyes looked very alert, but as before, afraid. It didn't fit the huge man. She guessed he'd had a bad experience with a dog in the past.

Skitch barked once and then growled more. Behind her, she felt someone rush outside from within the hangar and knew it must be Dak. She was sure of it when he spoke.

"You all right, Cori?"

"Yeah. Just greeting our early morning visitor."

She didn't turn around, and he took a few steps and came abreast of her on her left. She could see his rifle pointed at the man.

"Who are you?" Dak asked. "And what do you want?"

"Like I told her, I was just curious who it was in my neck of the woods. I saw the plane all crashed up..."

He pointed again.

"Are you from around here?" Cori asked.

He nodded. "I live in Pine Crest. I'm the only one left."

Skitch growled more, and Cori could see his hackles were up and his teeth bared.

"Please, don't let your dog attack me. I meant no harm. I just haven't seen anyone in months."

Dak looked at Skitch, and then made a noise in his throat. Skitch immediately ceased his growling and sat back in the gravel. He whined once and then was silent, his tongue hanging out while he panted as if nothing were wrong. The man looked immediately relieved.

"Can I lower my arms now?" the man asked.

Dak nodded but kept the gun trained on him.

"I'm Trevor," the big man said. "Are you two going to stay here for a while?"

"There's five of us here," Dak said. "And probably not. We've got someplace to be."

Trevor nodded. "I figured. Since you were on a plane and all. What happened to it?"

"It quit on us, and we had to land pretty quick. This was the closest place." Dak glanced at Cori who had lowered her weapon. The man seemed okay to her.

"I'm Cori. This is Dak." She bent to Skitch at her feet and petted him. "This is Skitch."

"Good to meet you, folks. Sorry if I startled you. Sometimes my curious side gets the best of me. Hey, I've got some stew on the fire at my place. You're welcome to share it with me if you folks are hungry." He smiled, and it lit up his face.

Dak lowered his weapon. "You have enough for all of us?"

"Sure do. I got me a twelve-point yesterday. Made a big pot of venison stew."

"That was you late in the afternoon firing the gun?"

"Yep."

Noah came out with his rifle followed by Chet and Flynn. Cori smiled at them.

"It's all right, Dad. This is Trevor. He's the lone resident of Pine Bluff."

"Crest," Trevor corrected. "Pine Crest. Hell, I guess it doesn't matter. I could call it Trevor Town and nobody would care. Good to meet you, folks. I was just saying to your friends that I have a big pot of venison stew that's been simmering on the fire all night. You're welcome to share a bowl with me. I got corn-bread too."

"Well, the last time I had cornbread, people numbered in the millions," Noah said.

"Come on, then," Trevor said. "I'm only about a mile that way." He pointed to the north.

"Let us pack our things up, and we'll follow you."

"You can leave your stuff here. Nobody around to mess with it. I'm it." He grinned.

Noah looked at Chet who shrugged. Flynn scratched the bandage on his head and licked his lips.

"I'm starved," Flynn said. "All we had last night was that porridge crap."

"Lead the way," Noah said and slung his rifle over his shoulder.

"You can leave the weapons," Trevor said. "I'm harmless."

"We'll carry until we know you better," Noah said. "If you don't mind."

"Sure. Sure. Whatever you want. I'm just glad to have some company." He bent to pick up his own rifle and froze before grabbing it. "This all right?"

"Yep. Go slow," Dak said.

Trevor picked it up and rested it on his shoulder pointing it at the sky. He kept his hands away from the trigger.

"Follow me."

He turned and headed north. They followed him without

another word and trekked through the tall grass to a little opening in the woods that Cori hadn't noticed before. It looked well-worn, and she wondered if Trevor came here often. Maybe he hunted in the open space for pheasant and rabbits.

"Where are you folks from?" Trevor asked.

"Florida," Noah said.

"Really? I went to that big amusement park in Orlando once. Didn't like all the people. Never went back."

"You'd like it now," Cori said. "It's pretty much deserted."

"I guess you could say that about everywhere. We survived for quite a bit longer than the rest of the world, what with us kinda isolated up here on this mountain, but the germ eventually found us, and that's all it took. The town died out in a matter of weeks. I'm the only one who survived. I guess I'm immune to it."

Cori thought it typical of the world that of all the people in this town, only one survived. She'd been through plenty of small towns over the last months that were completely deserted. No survivors. Trevor must be a lonely guy.

Noah and Dak filled the quiet with questions of their own for Trevor, and he answered them without a complaint. Cori could tell he was just excited to have someone else to talk to.

They emerged out of the wooded area onto a street that looked deserted. A few houses here and there and then the main area of town came into view, shops and businesses lining both sides of the two-lane road. It was a cozy little town, nothing more than two-story buildings in this place and Cori wondered if it even had a grocery store. Or had folks been required to drive into a bigger town to load up on supplies?

Trevor led the way through an overgrown yard to the front door of a single-story clapboard house that looked as if it had been built over a hundred years ago. The south end of the house sagged on its foundation and looked about to collapse. As they climbed the stairs to the porch, the structure creaked and moaned. Cori hoped she wouldn't fall through the old wood.

"It's not much, but I call it home," Trevor said. "I guess I coulda moved into one of the fancier places, but it just didn't seem right. I've lived here my whole life anyway. It was my ma and pa's before."

He held the door open, and Cori followed them in last, nodding to Trevor as he smiled at her. He smelled of unwashed clothes and sweat. The man definitely needed a bath, but she could forgive him if the stew were as good as it smelled as she walked in.

He shut the door and squeezed past them all, leading them to the small kitchen in the middle of the structure. The furniture was old and worn, the couch stained at the center with something that looked like old blood, but it really could have been anything. The chair that sat next to it had one of its legs cut off, and it was supported by an old log. In the kitchen, a small table sat by the lone window that looked out on the town, two simple chairs tucked in tight to it. A big pot sat on the gas stove, and Trevor went to it and lifted the lid off. The smell that filled the kitchen was heavenly, and Cori knew it was going to be a good day.

Trevor set about grabbing bowls and spoons from his cupboards and ladled big helpings of the stew into the bowls, passing them out as he made small talk. Cori took a bite of hers and grinned.

"Good," she said. "Really good."

"Thank you," Trevor said, as the others nodded in agreement, filling their mouths with the thick stew. He watched them eat with a weird grin on his face.

"You're not having any?" Cori asked.

"I already ate this morning," Trevor said, the weird grin staying on his face as his eyes moved from one person to the next. She kind of got a strange vibe coming off of him but pushed it to the back of her mind as the flavor of the stew overtook all her other senses.

They grabbed big hunks of cornbread out of a cast iron pan, and Cori was sure it tasted just like her grandma's. Too bad he didn't have any butter, but she couldn't complain. It was the best meal she'd had in a long time.

After they finished, Cori asked if he had a bathroom and he pointed down a hallway that led off of the kitchen.

"The water still runs, so you can flush it. Sorry, it's probably a mess in there. It's just me in this house." Trevor gave a funny smile, and she thought it typical of a bachelor to have a messy house.

She found the bathroom in the middle of the hall and agreed with his assessment of it. It was cluttered with dirty towels, clothes, boots, old newspapers and magazines, and a few feminine articles that made her wonder how long ago his mother had lived here. She picked up a box of tampons and noticed that several were missing. She put it back down on the small counter and thought it odd that an older woman who had been surely past menopause still needed tampons.

She used the toilet and sure enough, it flushed with a woosh of clean water. He must have a well or something. As she studied the things scattered around the room, she heard what sounded like a muffled voice. She paused and listened closely. She thought she heard it again and looked toward the closed door. She opened it and turned down the hallway that led deeper into the house. She listened closely but didn't hear anything again. At the end of the hallway, a door sat closed to her left, and another bigger door stood in front of her. It was made with sturdy wood and looked heavy. It was also padlocked with a fairly new and shiny lock that was bigger than her hand. She reached up and tested it—it was securely latched and not going anywhere. She heard the muffled voice again to her left and turned to the other door and tried it. It opened to a small utility closet that held a water heater. It made a squealing noise directly in front of her as the gas burner ignited. She shook her head to herself and closed the door.

Trevor was standing behind it in the hallway looking a bit angry in the low light. She jumped.

"I heard a noise," she said.

"The water heater squeals when it heats up." He studied her, and she was definitely picking up an uncomfortable vibe from him. He blocked her way with his big mass, and she could smell his unwashed body again, overwhelming in the tight space.

"I guessed. Sorry. I didn't mean to pry."

He stared at her hard and then smiled. "No problem. My place is always open and welcome. Did you find the bathroom?"

"Yes. Thank you. You have hot water?"

"I do."

"You don't know what I've give for a hot shower."

"You're welcome any time you'd like. I promise I won't peek."

She thought that an odd thing to say and suddenly felt like his eyes were all over her. She crossed her arms across her breasts and cleared her throat.

"Well, I better get back to the group. I'm sure they are anxious to get back to the airfield and work on the plane."

She had no idea what her dad's plans were for the morning, but she didn't want to stand here in this cramped hallway any longer with Trevor.

He nodded, turned, and walked back to the kitchen. She followed and glanced at Dak as she entered. He looked comfortable and didn't seem to acknowledge the look she was giving him.

"Well, thank you for the great meal," Noah said. "It's much appreciated. We better get out of your hair and head back to the airfield. I want to strip what I can out of the airplane before we head out."

"You're moving on already?" Trevor asked, looking disappointed.

"We're kind of on a mission," Cori said.

"What kind of mission?"

"We're tracking down my daughter," Noah said. "We've got a long way to go, and we want to keep moving. But we really appreciate the hospitality."

"You sure you don't want to stay in town a bit longer? I've got cake in the cupboard. And eggs from my chickens. I bet you haven't had cake in forever."

Noah grinned, and Cori could tell he was holding back a laugh.

"As good as that sounds," Noah said, "we really have to keep moving. Thank you, though."

Noah made to head out as Dak and Flynn and Chet grabbed up their weapons. Cori went to hers and slung it over her shoulder.

"Thank you again," Cori said. "It was yummy."

"Sure," Trevor said, the disappointment in his voice clearly evident. He looked like a lost giant boy standing there in the small kitchen.

They headed out, and he watched them head back down the street from his rickety porch. Cori turned back once, and he waved. She waved back and then he moved inside. She turned to Dak.

"He was kinda weird."

"I thought he was a nice guy. Very good cook."

"It was good. Still, I kind of got some creepy looks from him."

"What do you mean?"

"When I was back in the bathroom, I thought I heard a

voice, so I looked around. He surprised me and made a few weird comments. Plus, he kept staring at me."

"Like how?"

"You know. At my breasts and stuff."

Dak grinned. "You are pretty hot. Most guys would stare. As a matter of fact, as lonely as he is, I'd be surprised if he didn't stare."

"Still..."

"I wouldn't worry about it. He's harmless. Besides, we're leaving this place in our wake as soon as we can."

"Good. I want to get to Michalla as fast as we can."

Cori bumped into her dad, and she looked up. A boy of about eight stood in the road a few yards ahead of them. His dirty and disheveled hair hung in greasy clumps, and his clothes looked like torn rags that barely covered him. He had one tennis shoe on his right foot and a flip-flop on the other. He carried a small backpack in his hand that was in the shape of a monkey. Cori started to open her mouth and take a step toward him, but he spoke first in a low whisper.

"He has my mom."

Then, his eyes focused behind them and grew wide and afraid. He hesitated only a second and then bolted off into the woods next to the road.

"Hey!" Cori shouted after him, but he was gone.

Cori turned behind her and caught a glimpse of Trevor moving back inside his home. Cori moved toward the dense woods where the boy had disappeared and stared.

"What the hell?"

9

Autumn Leyshon went to the pretty blonde lying on the dirt floor of her prison and touched her face.

Cool. Not cold, but certainly not warm. The girl breathed shallow and slow, her lips slightly apart as the air continued to move in and out of her lungs. Good. At least she still lived. One other time, the bastard upstairs had done the same thing with another woman, and the poor thing had died right there on the floor. He'd left the body in with Autumn for two whole days. Sick son-of-a-bitch.

He liked to poison them. Some kind of drug he'd found at Pierce's Pharmacy on Main Street. A little gift from Lance Pierce himself as a leftover of the pandemic. He'd used it on Autumn herself back at the beginning, and she had survived. Too bad the other had not. She only hoped this one would live.

The blonde moaned and rolled over onto her back, her eyes fluttering up at the lone sixty-watt bare bulb that hung from the low ceiling in Autumn's prison. Then she lay still again. Autumn stood and went back over to her bed and sat on the edge of it. It had been a long time since she'd had another person to talk to. If the pretty girl survived, she was sure they would be fast friends. Or, at least friendly, and that would definitely be an improvement from her current conditions with Trevor.

She hated thinking his name. Never spoke it unless she had to. And certainly never used it in any positive way. The name represented evil to her. An evil she could never have imagined existed. He had taken her prisoner as the last of the residents in Pine Crest had succumbed to the virus. Taken her right from her own bed. Taken her from her son. And for that, she would always hate him. He claimed to love her, but if this was how you treated the one you loved, she didn't want to know what he'd do if he fell out of love with her.

He loved her. He told her almost every day. Had loved her from afar for years even before the world ended. She remembered him coming into the diner to sit at her table and thought him pleasant and a good tipper. Lonely, for sure, but not a psychopath. Too bad her judgment of him back then had been so off. He was as crazy as they come. And physically terrifying in his size. The funny thing was he had yet to touch her. At least in any sexual way. She was glad for that but wondered what purpose he had in keeping her locked up down in his basement. In this hell. She looked over at the marks on the beam above the small sink and counted them in her head. 182. 182 days he'd kept her down here. 182 days since she'd seen the sun. 182 days since she'd seen her boy. She didn't even know if he was still alive.

A single tear rolled down her cheek, and she wiped it away with a hand that shook. She wrapped the one thin blanket she had around her shoulders and scooted back in the bed to huddle against the wall. She watched the pretty girl. Air moving in and out of her lungs. Slowly. But definitely still breathing. She could only hope the girl would live.

~

CORI DREAMED of a cool forest floor. The damp leaves sticking to her hair and the smell of earth and foliage strong in her nostrils. It was a good smell. A nice relaxing feeling of peace and tranquility.

Then a wave of nausea struck her like a wall of death. She sat up and vomited all over the floor next to her. She retched and retched for what seemed an eternity and then caught her breath as the wave of nausea subsided. She felt cool hands on her arms and thought Dak could even watch her throw up and still love her. She looked up and saw a face she didn't recognize in the low light.

"Who...?"

But her voice failed her, and she coughed. She tried to pull away from the face and hands, but she was so weak. So weak.

"Take it easy," a woman's voice said in her ear. "You've been drugged. You'll feel better tomorrow. Just rest."

"Where am I?"

"You're in his house. The basement."

"Whose house?"

Then she remembered. Back at the airfield, Cori couldn't get the picture of the boy out of her head. Nobody else seemed concerned by the fact that Trevor had not been truthful. That he wasn't alone in the town. In fact, a little boy that appeared to be in bad shape roamed the streets and woods and claimed to have a mother that was with Trevor.

On the way back to the hangar, Cori had tried to argue with her dad and Dak that they needed to go back to Trevor's and confront him. If he really did have some woman in his house, was she being held against her will? Or was she just a terrible mother who had abandoned her child for the only man left alive in town?

"It's not our business," Dak had said.

"The boy made it our business," Cori said. "You heard him."

"That's the thing. I didn't hear him. He spoke so softly that he could have said just about anything and I might have interpreted it differently."

"But you didn't. We all heard what he said, 'He has my mom,' right? That's what I heard. And when I was back in the bathroom, I did hear something. I know it now. It was a voice, muffled and faint, shouting out."

"You said it was the water heater."

"Yes, that's what made the most sense at the time because that's what Trevor said it was."

Then her memory became fuzzy. She had been tired. So tired. And so had everyone else. She had laid down on her pallet, and then...nothing. Until she woke from her pleasant dream and vomited all over the ground. Some hazy memories of a big man appearing in the hangar and somebody lifting her up and then floating. Floating away into nothingness.

Cori studied the woman in front of her more closely and felt like she should know her. Red hair, green eyes that were so beautiful they didn't belong in these surroundings or with the sad face that held them, and a small and dainty nose that completed the face that most would call pretty. She wore plain, shabby clothes that hung off of her thin frame, making it look like she wore a sack with some legs. The woman stared back at Cori unblinking and then she smiled. Her whole face lit up with that smile and Cori couldn't look away.

"You're his mother," Cori whispered.

The woman grew excited. "My boy. My Eric. You saw him? He's alive?" She grabbed Cori's upper arm in a vice-like grip and Cori must have made a face because the woman eased up, but still remained intense in front of her.

Cori nodded.

"Black hair, brown eyes," the woman said. "He'd be nine, now. Kind of short for a nine-year-old. Very polite and friendly."

"He didn't stick around long enough to be polite. He said, 'He has my mom,' and then ran off into the woods."

"But it was him? How was he? Did he look good? Has he been eating? Was he healthy? Are you sure it was him?"

"It had to be," Cori said. "Trevor told us he was the only living person in the town. But, it now appears he was not truthful. He looked dirty and a bit thin, but he seemed fit and healthy. I mean he ran away from us pretty fast."

The woman's face changed at the mention of Trevor's name, and she shook her head and made a noise in her throat.

"That man would lie to the Pope or God himself." The woman let Cori's arm go and stood up, moving to the lone chair in the small room. "What's your name?"

"Cori."

"Hello, Cori. I'm Autumn."

She stuck out her hand, and Cori shook it slowly. A silence settled between them, and Cori took the moment to look around. She was definitely in a basement. Concrete walls with wooden beams on the ceiling, dirt floor, and a dampness to the air. A single sink and toilet sat against the opposite wall. Behind her, a bed was pushed up against the wall. Autumn sat in the only chair in the room. A small armoire rested near the big oak door. She assumed it held Autumn's things, but then she saw the padlock on it and wondered what was inside. There were no windows and only a single, naked bulb hanging from the ceiling.

Cori tried to stand, but her legs felt like jelly, and she fell back to the floor in frustration. Autumn came over and helped her to the bed.

"You should rest. The poison is still in your system, and you're weak. Go ahead and lay down. I'll sit and keep an eye on you."

"What did he give me?"

"Did you eat something he made, like soup or a stew?"

Cori nodded. "Venison stew."

"That's how he does it. He puts it in the stew, and you eat more than you should. You can't taste it. At least I couldn't tell it was poisoned. He brought me soup, and I thought he was just being nice. There were only a few of us left at that time, and we all seemed to want to help each other."

"How long have you been down here? Do you even know?"

"182 days."

Cori felt her stomach lurch at that bit of information. She couldn't imagine being trapped in this dark room for six months. Her face must have given her thoughts away because Autumn grimaced and nodded.

"I can't believe it either. I tried to get away from him. Tried so many times. I wasn't strong enough, and he'd beat me afterward. Finally, I just gave in." Cori could see tears starting to form in her eyes. "He feeds me. Let's me take a shower once a week. But that's about it. He sits with me every day and talks to me. But I hate that time of day. He's a psychopath and talking to him makes me feel...lost. Like there is something wrong with me."

"What does he want from us?"

"I used to think it was companionship. But he seems happy with his loneliness. I now believe he just likes to keep things captive. He likes to be in control. To rule over his subjects. He doesn't ever touch me. At least not yet."

"My fiancé, Dak, won't like him taking me. Not one bit. He and my dad will come and get me."

"If they're not dead. They ate the same thing you did?"

Cori nodded, slowly, not liking the thought that Dak and her dad could be dead. "But I'm alive."

"He gave you a drug that helps to reverse the effects of the poison. Right when you arrived here. Your friends and father received no such drug."

Cori felt tears welling up in her eyes. "They're strong. They will survive. I know it."

Autumn said nothing for a long moment. "I hope so," but she didn't sound convincing, and Cori worried they would all die at the hands of Trevor. Why did they trust him? It's not like her small group just believes people. Especially the way things were in the world now. If they got out of this unscathed, she'd never trust anyone again. Thinking back on her first encounter with Trevor, it had been her that had lowered her guard first. He had seemed like a nice guy. A lonely, but friendly man.

Footsteps above her head caused her to look up, and she followed the sound of them as they moved across the ceiling. She looked at Autumn whose face had changed to one of fear and loathing. She shrank away from the sound and wrapped her arms around herself.

"He's coming," she whispered.

10

Dak rolled over and felt the bile rise in the back of his throat. He sat up and vomited all over his pallet. When he finished, he wiped his mouth with his hand and felt the fog in his brain try and return. He shook his head violently, and it didn't help. He felt drugged. Like when he'd gotten his wisdom teeth removed years ago, and he lay in a big dental chair as the sedation wore off. He didn't like that feeling.

He tried to focus on his surroundings, but things were blurry and fuzzy in his vision. He reached over to the spot where Cori should be and felt emptiness. He turned and saw that her bedding area was deserted. He searched the hangar, but with his vision going in and out of focus, he couldn't make out anything more than shapes.

His stomach lurched again, and only thick, ropy strings of yellow bile came up. He retched for a good five minutes and lay back when he finished. He gasped for air and couldn't understand why he was so weak. As he lay there, he heard someone else vomiting and wondered if they were all sick or something. More retching and the sound of vomiting continued behind him for what seemed an eternity. When it stopped, he called out.

"Whose sick? Is that you, Cori?"

"It's Noah. Man, I feel like crap. What the hell did I eat?"

Dak could hear him retching again and tried to sit up. The world spun crazily, and he sagged back down. It was like he had drank a whole fifth of vodka in just a few minutes. Had he gotten drunk? Is that what this was? Was he hungover? Where was Cori? Did they all get drunk? He couldn't remember.

He felt himself going in and out of consciousness and couldn't tell how much time had passed since he last threw up. He tried sitting up again and made it, the dizziness lasting only a few seconds as his world came into focus. He was in the hangar, on his pallet, the fire in the center of their group cold and dormant. Noah lay a few spaces over as did Chet and Flynn. Cori was nowhere to be seen.

"Cor! Cori!"

Nothing. The only sound was the wind moaning through the rafters of the hangar. He went to stand and staggered crashing to his knees as the dizziness returned. Someone moaned nearby and then vomited. He turned to see Chet on his elbow, puking his guts out. He turned away.

What the hell was going on?

Dak staggered over to Noah and looked down at him. His eyes were closed as his chest rose up and down and he was about to bend over and shake him awake when Chet spoke.

"Are you sick too?"

Dak nodded. "Yeah. I puked all over my pallet. So did Noah. I can't find Cori. Do you know where Cori is?"

Chet shook his head, no. "I don't remember a thing. I don't even remember how I got here. The last thing I remember is that big dude and his stew. It must have been bad or something. Made us all sick."

Dak remembered the stew. It had been good. Really good.

And they had all eaten their fill. Then his memory failed him. He couldn't seem to figure out how they all got back to the airfield. Had it been daylight still? Night time? What day was it now? How long had they been out?

He stumbled over to the small office at the back of the hangar and peered inside. Nothing. No Cori. He made it to the broken hangar door and stepped over it into the sunlight. He shielded his eyes as the light bore daggers into his aching head. He scanned the area but could find no sign of Cori.

"Cori!" He shouted at the top of his lungs. "Cori! Where are you?!"

Nothing.

He heard Noah cough behind him and stepped back inside the hangar. His strength seem to leave him all at once, and he sagged to the ground next to Noah. Noah rubbed his face with his hands as he sat up and Dak could tell he was having a hard time focusing on him.

"Noah. Where's your daughter?"

"What?"

"Cori. I can't find Cori. Do you know where she is?"

"What?"

Dak reached out and shook him. "Noah! Come on! Snap out of it! I can't find Cori."

Noah shook his head and tried to stand, but stumbled and went back down.

"I feel like I'm drugged. Or drunk. Did you say Cori's missing?"

"Yes. I can't find her. She's not here or anywhere I can see outside."

"Are you sick too?"

"Yes, we all are. I think the stew that guy Trevor fed us was bad. Food poisoning or something."

"This is not food poisoning," Noah said, his eyes narrowing

and finally finding focus as he studied Dak. "If I were a betting man, I'd say that son-of-a-bitch drugged us."

Dak thought about it, and it made sense. He was feeling way worse than any other time he'd eaten something bad. It was the fog and weakness that was different. He could hardly function.

"Cori could have wandered off into the field or the woods if she were delirious with the drug," Noah said. "We have to find her."

He stood, weaved a little on his legs, and then seemed to steady himself. Dak stood too.

"I'll look in the other hangars and the woods; you take the airfield."

Noah nodded, and they both moved outside the hangar and separated. Dak headed for the closest hangar, his stumbling, shuffling, walk a sign that whatever had happened at the hands of Trevor was still affecting him.

CORI LISTENED as the sounds of locks and deadbolts being undone came from the other side of the big oak door, and then it swung open. Trevor stood in the open doorway, a set of keys in his hand and a tray in the other. On the tray, two glasses sat filled with some kind of white liquid. She found his face and saw him grinning at her. He stepped into the room and closed the door behind him.

"Glad to see you're awake," he said to her. "Feeling okay?"

"No," Cori said. "I'm not. Not one bit. And if you know what's good for you, you'll let me out of here right now. Dak is not going to be as forgiving as I am when he figures out what's happened to me."

"He's dead."

The two words hit her like fists to the gut. She felt herself gasp and then her world seemed to spin and come apart. She heard herself moan and then found Autumn next to her, pulling her to her. She let the woman hold her as Trevor set the tray down on the edge of the sink. He picked up one of the glasses and thrust it out to her.

"Drink this. It will help."

Cori only stared at it, her senses slowly returning to some semblance of normal after the shock he had dealt her. How could her Dak be dead? And her dad? It couldn't be true. She knew in her heart that it couldn't be true.

"How?"

"How what?" Trevor asked.

"How do you know he's dead?"

"The drug I gave you all is pretty potent. The only reason you're alive is because I gave you an antidote to it. Narcan. It reverses the effect of the drug pretty quickly." He smiled again, and it made her shiver with disgust.

"What do you want?"

He set the glass back down on the tray and stood there by the sink, staring at her. She wondered if he'd heard her. She was about to ask again when he spoke.

"It's not what I want. It's what you want. You'll realize that soon enough."

"I want out of here. Let me go."

"No, you don't." He chuckled, licked his lips, and then ran a grimy hand through his long hair. She could smell his body odor as it filled the room. "Your desires at this moment only address the way you feel in the present. When things have calmed down, you'll find that what you really want is here." He turned to the tray again and picked up both glasses. He handed one to Autumn, who took it without hesitation and held the other out for Cori. She didn't move.

"Drink," he said.

Autumn did immediately as she was told and Cori could hear her gulping down whatever was in the glass. She turned to Autumn who took a gasping breath as the white liquid dribbled down her chin. Her glass was empty. She nodded to Cori. Cori turned back to Trevor and reached out a hand that shook. He put the glass in her fingers and then she threw the glass as hard as she could at him. It struck him in the chest, and the white stuff splashed over his beard and face as the glass crashed to the dirt floor. It did not break.

She felt Autumn shrink away from her but kept her focus on Trevor. He looked down at his wet shirt and when he looked back up his face had become something she didn't recognize. He roared in anger and quicker than she could have imagined, she was being lifted up off the bed by her throat, his hand squeezing painfully around her windpipe. He held her up with one hand above the floor, her feet kicking feebly as she tried to gain her footing. He pulled her face to within an inch of his, his sour breath blowing on her, and then tossed her into the armoire as if she were a bag of laundry. She hit it with a force that cracked the old piece of furniture, stars appearing in her vision as she hit the floor, and then his boot found her ribs, and she felt something give. The pain was worse than anything she'd ever felt before, and as she tried to cry out, he grabbed her by the hair and flung her into the toilet. She struck the porcelain bowl with her head, and the world spun. She felt him move out of the room and as her senses came back to her and the pain returned, she heard the door slam shut and the locks snick back into place. Autumn came to her and pulled her to her. She rocked her in her arms as Cori's tears started to flow.

DAK FOUND the first of the other two hangars locked with a padlock. He grabbed it and tugged, but it didn't budge. At least she couldn't be in there unless there was another way in. He circled the building and found a door at the rear, but it was locked as well. The lone window was grimy and hard to see through, but he searched through it and did not see her. There was a plane inside, but it was too dark for Dak to determine what kind of shape it was in or even what model.

He stumbled to the last hangar, his energy waning as the nausea returned. He retched into the grass, collapsing to his hands and knees as the wave took over. The only thing left inside of him was the yellow bile that he'd seen before. When he finished, he stood shakily and searched for Noah in the distance. He found him by the TBM, but he was alone.

At the last hangar, the big sliding door was slightly ajar, and he pushed it on rusty wheels the rest of the way open. It screeched in protest, the sound carrying across the open space behind him. Inside, a biplane sat, its red paint gleaming in the sunlight that now streamed in. It looked almost brand new except for the dust covering its surface. He ignored it and moved inside. Cori was nowhere to be seen. He found the skeletal remains of what must be the owner sitting in a chair behind the lone desk in the little room in the back. The smell that filled the room caused his stomach to lurch again. He gagged and backpedaled out of the room and back out into the open air outside the hangar. He watched as Noah moved through the tall grass searching for any sign of Cori.

"Anything?!" Dak yelled.

"No!" Noah yelled back.

They met in the grass and Dak decided that Noah looked as bad as he felt. His ashen face had sweat running down it despite the cool air. Whatever they had all eaten with the stew sure had done a number on them. Dak suddenly felt weaker, and his legs shook. He thought he was going down, but Noah reached out and steadied him.

"I did the same thing," Noah said. "Out by the TBM. I had to sit for a minute. Maybe you should rest."

"No. I'm okay."

They heard a shout and looked back at Chet in the doorway of the hangar waving his arm above his head. Dak looked at Noah, and they both headed in Chet's direction. When they arrived, he was leaning against the doorway to the hangar, breathing hard and looking as pale and gray as a man of his color could look. He lifted his head as they approached.

"Flynn is dead," he said.

"Are you sure?" Noah asked.

"Go check for yourself."

Noah and Dak went inside and found Flynn face up on his pallet. His half-open eyelids and slack mouth gave Dak a sinking feeling in his gut. Dak could tell all the muscles in his body were flaccid. Noah knelt next to him and felt for a pulse at his neck. He stayed that way for a good minute and then looked up at Dak, shaking his head.

"Damn," Dak said.

Chet had come back in and stood weaving on his feet by the little circle of pallets. He made a weird noise and then sagged onto the nearest one.

"What the hell did that bastard do to us?" Noah said. "When I see him, I'm going to beat him bloody."

"What if he has Cori?" Dak said. "We have to go now and get her back."

"I agree. But we're in no shape to fight. Look at us. We can barely stand or walk. You look like you're about to keel right over and I'm sure I look the same."

"We can't just sit here. I'm going. If you can't, I understand, but she could be in real trouble."

Noah nodded, went to his rifle next to his bed, and picked it up. He checked it and seemed satisfied. "I'm going with you."

"Me too," Chet said.

"What about Flynn's body?" Noah asked.

"It's not going anywhere," Dak said. "We'll attend to him after we get Cori back."

Noah stared down at his friend and nodded slowly. "Terrina's going to be lost without him."

11

Trevor's house looked abandoned and silent.

Dak blinked in the sunlight, his head pounding and the sweat beading up on his scalp. He felt horrible, but he couldn't let that keep him from the task at hand.

He was across the street from Trevor's house in an old storefront, the big plate glass window of the store grimy and covered in dirt and dust. He knelt behind a counter and studied the house for movement and signs of the big man. Noah was in the shop next to him. Dak presumed he was doing the same as him, watching and waiting for Dak to make the move on the house. Chet had worked himself around to the back of the house and would move in when he heard the action begin.

If it began. Dak was beginning to wonder if the big man had already moved on with Cori and the woman the kid had mentioned yesterday. Dak tried to focus, but his vision kept blurring, and he shook his head trying to clear it. He couldn't remember if they had seen the kid yesterday or the day before. How many days had he laid on his pallet passed out? He had no judge of time at this point, and for all he knew, it could have been a week.

Movement caught his eye, and he watched as the front door opened and Trevor stepped out onto the porch, a big double-barrel shotgun in his hands. He scanned his surroundings but didn't seem to find anything that alarmed him. He went back inside, the door slapping shut behind him on the rusty spring. Dak clenched his teeth and stood.

The sudden change in his stance made him feel light-headed, and he waited until his blood pressure returned to normal. He moved out of the store, walked quickly across the street, bounded up the steps onto the porch, and kicked in the door. He heard Noah running up behind him as he brought his M4 up and moved inside.

He paused, letting his eyes adjust to the gloom of the front room, his head on a swivel trying to see everything at once. He remembered the beat-up furniture and knick-knacks of the cluttered room and let his focus settle on the hallway leading to the kitchen. This room was void of any other human beings save him and Noah.

Noah pointed silently to the hall, and Dak nodded, keeping his weapon up as he moved across the room. The floor creaked beneath his feet, and the smell of the stew from their prior visit filled his nostrils as he moved closer to the kitchen. It nause-ated him, and he swallowed repeatedly remembering the taste of it as it had come back up this morning. He shook his head, trying to keep things focused on finding Cori.

In the kitchen, the space was empty, and Dak was begin-ning to think the man had fled the house. On their last visit here, Dak had seen the bathroom and the one other padlocked door but had not seen any of the other rooms. He pushed past the kitchen down the hallway toward the bathroom, found it empty as well, and then stood in front of the big padlocked door that filled that end of the hall.

Only the padlock was hanging open on its hasp. Dak nodded to it, and Noah nodded back. He pulled on the door, and it swung open on big heavy hinges. Beyond the door, a dark space showed them nothing but stairs leading downward. Dak moved in.

The stairs creaked and moaned as he made his way down— Noah right behind—as his eyes adjusted to this even darker area of the house. At the bottom of the stairs, a small landing filled the space, and then another huge door with light seeping out from underneath. Dak pushed it open and found himself face-to-face with the big man.

And he was not alone.

Dak felt all hope leave him as he took in the scene. Trevor stood grinning beneath a single bare bulb, Cori next to him with Trevor's big double barrel shotgun pressed to her temple, his finger on the trigger. She didn't look frightened, only angry. And then Dak saw the bruise on her cheek and rage filled him as he tightened his grip on the M4 sighting down it at Trevor's head. Noah cursed beneath his breath beside him.

Trevor made a noise that could have been a single laugh, but to Dak it sounded more like a cough. The smile never left his face, and he showed no fear or apprehension. In fact, he pressed the barrel of his shotgun harder into Cori's temple. There was another woman in the room. She sat on the lone bed, her back pressed up against the wall and her legs drawn up to her chest. Her terror-filled eyes were a distraction that Dak decided he didn't need. He focused on Cori and the giant of a man holding her.

Dak spoke first.

"Let her go."

"Now, why would I do that?" The smile that seemed to never leave his face only fueled the anger seething through Dak's body.

"We've got two rifles pointed at your head, that's why. You harm her. You die."

"It seems to me that she's a bit more important to you than

your ability to dispose of me after I remove her pretty head with two big rounds of buckshot. You lower your weapons, turn around, and walk back up those stairs and out of my house." His grin left his face. "And she lives."

Dak kept his gun trained on Trevor's head as the big man's words worked through his brain. Dak knew that the man was right. There was no way he could get the jump on him before he pulled the trigger and ended Cori's life and the life of their unborn child right there in front of him. And he couldn't let that happen.

"Lower your weapons," Trevor said softly. "Now."

Dak hesitated a brief second and then lowered his rifle. He felt Noah do the same.

"Dak. No," Cori said.

Dak stared into Cori's eyes and felt the despair in her fill his soul with anguish. He had failed. He'd walked blindly into a situation that was hopeless. He'd been a fool to think he could just shoot his way into this man's house and rescue the damsel in distress. The only thing he'd done is endanger the life of the one person he cared for most in this world.

"If you think we're just going to let you keep her..." Dak's words sounded empty, even to him.

"Or what?" Trevor mocked. "I'm holding all the cards here."

"We'll be back."

"Oh, I'm sure you will. That's why we're going to make a little deal. Right here and now."

"What kind of deal?" Noah asked. "That's my daughter's head you're holding a shotgun against, and I'm not about to deal her life away."

"Who's the pilot?"

The question confused Dak for a second and then he understood. "He is." Dak nodded to Noah. "You killed our other pilot with that poison you fed us."

Trevor's grin was back, and he laughed once. "You liked it, huh?" Then the grin left him. "It was supposed to kill you."

"We survived."

"Here's the deal. You fly me and my bride," he tilted his head toward the woman on the bed who flinched at the suggestion that she was anything other than another prisoner of his, "out of this damn town and to Savannah and this pretty little thing lives."

"What else?" Noah asked.

"That's it. It's pretty simple. You get me to where I want to go, and she's yours. Good as new."

Dak studied the man and felt in his heart that he was lying. That he'd kill Cori after all this was done and then he'd kill them all. Without hesitation. The problem was, Dak really had no other choice at the moment, and it would buy him some time to figure out a way to free Cori. The other problem was they didn't have a plane that worked.

"You fly me on that fancy plane in the field, and I set her free."

"The plane is a wreck," Noah said. "It's no longer airworthy. She won't fly."

"Then you get one of those other ones in the hangars flying and do what I ask."

"There are airworthy aircraft in the hangars?"

Trevor shrugged. "I've seen them. It's up to you to get them flying."

"What if we can't?"

"Then you get her back in a pine box."

She squirmed in his grasp, and he pulled her closer. "Now, move out. Don't come back until you have me a way out of this crap town."

Dak stared into Cori's eyes and nodded once to her. She looked lost. That him leaving her with this monster was a thing she would never forgive him for. It broke his heart, but he had no other choice. He turned and pushed Noah to go. He resisted and then finally said, "We'll be back, baby. I promise."

Trevor only laughed and watched as they moved up the stairs and out into the sunlight.

Dak shook with frustration and anger at his inability to get Cori away from him. Chet emerged from the side of the house and walked over.

"What happened?" he asked.

"The man's a psycho," Noah said. "And we have to find a way to put him down."

Chet eyed them both but didn't say another word.

CORI USED the sink to wash the tears from her face and then realized there was no towel to dry her skin. She shook her head and let the water drip from her face. She turned to Autumn and found the woman crying silently to herself. Cori felt weak. Weak and alone, despite Autumn sitting in the same room with her. Ever since Trevor had made it clear that he intended to take her to Savannah with him, she'd done nothing but cry. Cori had tried to talk to her, but she'd remained silent. She wondered if the woman had finally gone off the deep end.

Cori sat on the dirt floor, her back up against the concrete wall, and tried to relax. When Autumn spoke, her voice sounded haunted and alone.

"My boy will be all by himself."

Cori had forgotten about the little boy who had told them about his mom. A sadness filled her that even made her own fear seem a nuisance. True, the boy had been on his own since Trevor had made Autumn a prisoner, but the finality of that loneliness when Trevor took her away seemed brutal in its cruelty. How could he leave a nine-year-old to fend for himself?

Cori didn't know what to say to Autumn. She knew the woman to be right, and there were no words that would make a difference. So, she stood, and went to her on the bed and pulled her close, holding her in her arms.

"I won't go with him," she finally said. "I'll die first. I can't stand living knowing that I left my Eric alone to die in this deserted town."

"Dak will find a way. He'll find a way to get us away from Trevor."

The mention of the man's name made Autumn flinch, and she pulled away from Cori.

"I deserve to die. I'm a failure as a mother and human being."

"You can't believe that. You're a victim here. There's no way you could have known that Trevor was a madman. And he took you away from your son. You had no choice in the matter."

"I could have fought him. I could have done something to get away from him. I was just afraid."

"He's a big man, Autumn. I can't stand up to him. Neither could you. You have no one to blame but Trevor himself. He did this to you."

Autumn looked into Cori's eyes, and Cori could see that the woman didn't believe the words Cori spoke. She had it in her head that she was at fault. And nothing Cori could say would change that perception.

THEY BURIED Flynn under a big maple tree at the edge of the field. Noah said a few words and then pounded a marker into the ground at the head of the grave. Dak had liked the man. He had been a good father and a skillful pilot. He wondered what would happen to Terrina now that her father was no longer around to take care of her. At least she was with good people back at the Cape, and Brenna, with her medical skills, would keep her healthy. At least as healthy as she could. They'd have to find a way to get her Insulin, but he knew that Brenna would do whatever it took to keep the girl alive.

Walking back to the hangar, Dak studied the other buildings that they had yet to explore and wondered if they'd find an airplane they could fly. Noah must have been thinking the same thing because he spoke his mind.

"There's no way I'm flying that man anywhere, much less to a place he wants me to take him. He's going to kill Cori no matter what we do, so I want to take him out before he has that chance."

"You'd be putting your own daughter's life at risk," Chet said.

"Do you believe a word that comes out of that man's mouth? He already tried to poison us all and actually succeeded in killing Flynn. For that reason alone, he deserves to die. Cori's at risk no matter what we do now."

"I agree," Dak said. "I don't think he has any intentions of letting any of us live once we do what he wants us to do. Besides, this whole thing with Savannah doesn't make sense. If he wanted us to take him to Savannah in the first place, why would he try and kill us with that poisoned stew?"

"True," Chet said. "It doesn't add up. I wonder what his end-game really is?"

"It's to keep Cori for himself and to kill us off, so we're no threat to him and his little harem of girls." Dak couldn't help but grow angry at the thought of the big man violating Cori or any other woman. "If he touches her..."

"I won't let him," Noah said. "This ends today. Come on. I have an idea."

Dak followed him to the hangar and realized he'd be willing to do anything to make sure Cori was okay. Even if that meant sacrificing himself so she'd live. Skitch ran up to them as they approached and Dak rubbed his ears.

"I'm glad you're not worried, boy," Dak said. "I think you're the only sane one around here."

Skitch wagged his tail and looked happy. Too bad Dak couldn't feel the same.

12

"Get out here!"

Dak stood in the street in front of Trevor's house and looked up and down the deserted main thoroughfare. He called out again, adjusting his rifle across his chest.

"Get out here! Now!"

The door opened on squeaky hinges, and the big man walked out carrying his double barrel. The spring on the door caused it to slam shut behind him. Dak knew Noah and Chet were in their hiding places, but he still felt exposed out on the road. Still, it's what needed to be done.

"Where's Cori?"

"She's in the cellar. She's safe." Trevor hefted the shotgun and raised it to his shoulder. He pointed it at Dak's middle. "Why are you here?"

"You said you wanted a ride. We've got a ride. Bring Cori and yourself to the airfield, and we'll go from there."

"That was awful quick. You've only been gone two hours. How could you get a plane ready to fly in two hours? Especially since they've been sittin' for months."

"I'm not the pilot. You'll have to ask Noah. I'm just the messenger."

Trevor eyed him but didn't lower the shotgun.

"Stop pointing that thing at me," Dak said. "We've done what you asked, and we're ready to take you where you want to go. Now, hold up to your end of the bargain."

Trevor lowered the gun and finally grinned. Dak had the thought flash in his head that he could take a shot at him right now. End this. But what if he missed? That shotgun could do a lot of damage if he got the chance to point it at him and pull the trigger. Then, what would happen to Cori?

"I'll be there with the girls in one hour." Trevor said nothing else, turned, and moved back inside.

Dak nodded to himself and walked away from the house toward the airfield.

The boy suddenly appeared from behind some trees and stood in the road. Dak froze.

"Where are you taking him?" the boy asked in a soft voice.

"Nowhere."

"You said you were ready to take him where he wanted to go."

"He asked us to take him to Savannah."

"You can't take my mom away. You can't." The boy looked about to lose it.

"He asked us to take him to Savannah," Dak repeated. "He thinks that's what's going to happen. But we have other plans."

The boy studied him for a full minute. Then he spoke four words.

"I want to help."

DAK WAITED inside the hangar as Trevor approached with Cori and the other woman. He had them walking in a single-file line with the shotgun pointed at their backs, and a pistol in a holster at his hip. Coward. The late afternoon light caused the leaves to shimmer in the distance—blinking gold, then red, then gold again like little holiday lights. The vision would have been beautiful if not for the situation. Dak tightened his sweating hands on the rifle and took a deep breath.

This was going to work.

Trevor walked up to the hangar with the broken door, looked inside, found it empty, and then scanned the surrounding airport. He found the open door of the hangar that Dak now occupied and made his way over just as Dak knew he would.

Chet was at the back of the hangar in its own little office, hunkered down behind the wall. Noah was positioned behind a tractor, his sniper rifle resting atop the faded red motor housing, open field between him and the door of the building that Trevor moved toward. If things went as planned, the big man would be down, and Cori and the woman would be free of him.

If it all went to plan.

Behind Dak, an old Cessna 172 sat on flat and rotten tires, its windows and paint grimy with ages of dirt. When they had opened the hangar and found the plane inside, they could tell no one had been in the structure or taken care of the plane in at least a decade. Probably more.

As Trevor stopped in the hangar doorway and looked inside, his face changed from that of satisfaction to a kind of confusion and then anger as he looked over the plane. He pulled Cori to him and pressed the barrel of the shotgun to her head. The other woman he called over to him, and she obeyed, standing on the other side.

"What is this?" Trevor asked. "This plane ain't ready to fly. Hell, it ain't even ready to roll. I couldn't even drive it to town."

"Change of plans," Dak said. "You give us Cori and Autumn, and you live."

Dak glanced at Cori who was doing her best to remain calm and brave. She stood tall and proud, her head held high and her eyes focused on Dak. The presence of the gun against her temple seemed only a nuisance.

Good girl, Dak thought.

The Autumn woman was another story. The tears that tracked down her face made her look crazy. She trembled next to Trevor and shrank in on herself, like a child who had been scolded and knew that what came next would be bad. She might be a problem.

"You forget, boy. I've got the gun against her head. If she so much as breaths funny, or you give me the willies, her head will be nothing but a red cloud of blood and brains."

The image made Dak doubt what would happen, but only for an instant. Because things happened very quickly after that.

Trevor's face changed as his eyes moved to the right and followed the boy as he moved out from behind the airplane. Eric walked calmly over to Dak and stood next to him. Autumn's breath caught in her throat and then she made a move toward her son as the tears came harder. Trevor had to lower the gun from Cori's head to reach out and grab Autumn.

"Get back here, woman!"

Skitch bounded out from behind the plane and charged Trevor at a full run, his teeth barred and his deep growl clearly heard. Trevor froze for a couple of seconds, the fear in his eyes evident as the dog he'd forgotten all about bore down on him. As Skitch left the ground and leaped at Trevor's throat, he finally moved. Dak shouted.

"Cori!"

Dak sank to his knee, bringing up the M4, and watched with satisfaction as Cori understood and jumped to her right away from the big man. Trevor's shotgun was coming up as Skitch hit him hard, the sound of his snarling a scary thing for anyone. Trevor screamed as a shot rang out from outside, but

Noah missed wide, and the bullet smacked into the airframe next to Dak. Dak pulled the boy down to his knees and aimed down the M4's sites just as the shotgun went off, the blast inside the hangar deafening. Skitch sank his teeth into the soft flesh of Trevor's neck, and the man dropped the shotgun and fought against the German shepherd attacking him with the ferocity of a wild animal. He screamed again and pounded on the dog's back with his fists.

Autumn stood there, her hand up by her open mouth, the shock of all that was happening registering on her face. Then, she seemed to change in front of Dak's eyes. She calmly lowered her hand and took a step toward Trevor and Skitch. She reached out and pulled the pistol out of its holster on Trevor's hip and placed the barrel against his head. Without hesitation, she pulled the trigger, and his head exploded.

Skitch yipped, let go, and bolted away as Trevor's body sagged to the ground at Autumn's feet, the gun held steady in her outstretched arm. She turned slowly, found her son, and lowered the weapon. She went to Eric and took him in her arms where the boy gladly found safety and peace. Cori ran to Dak who pulled her to him as Skitch circled the small group, still worked up and anxious. Cori patted her leg for him to come to her and he approached, whining.

"Good boy! What a good boy!" She rubbed his head and sides and got him calmed down.

Chet came over with his rifle held at the ready as Noah ran up to the open hangar door. He lowered the sniper rifle and nodded to Dak.

It was over.

Cori was saddened at the loss of Flynn, his kind heart and love for his daughter his defining traits. She stood over the makeshift grave under the big tree and thought of Terrina. What would the girl do now without her father? They had all been concerned for the girl's welfare, but only considered turning back for a few minutes before dismissing the idea. They had their own mission to accomplish. Besides, Terrina was in good hands with a doctor to care for her and Kyla and Dex to keep her busy. Of course, she had no idea her father was gone and wouldn't know until Cori, and her little group returned. And that seemed to sadden Cori the most. There was nothing she could do about it.

Autumn approached, then hesitated and Cori could tell the woman was unsure if she was disturbing her. Cori reached out a hand and Autumn came over and smiled, taking it in hers.

"I'm so sorry about your friend."

"So am I. He was a good man."

"I feel like it's my fault. That all of you suffered because of me."

"It was all Trevor. You have to know that. He took you as a prisoner, kidnapped and poisoned me along with my friends. All because he was sick."

Autumn grew silent, looking around at the leaves turning to fall colors, the beauty something that was not lost on Cori either. A light breeze came up from the open field, and the leaves shimmered and rattled in the chill air.

"I'm not sure what I'm going to do now," Autumn said. "Eric and I are the only people left in this town, and it feels so lonely."

"You could come with us."

"Where are you going, exactly? We never got around to talking about why you're here."

"North Dakota. To reunite with my sister. We've come a long way to find her."

"North Dakota," Autumn said, softly. "It sounds so far away.

Still, it might be a new start for us. I don't want to be a burden, though. Your supplies..."

"We'll be fine. We gather what we need as we move from town to town. And we're good at hunting. I don't think you'll find yourself hungry."

"Have you ever lived up north?"

"No. Why?"

"Things are different in the winter. And winter is coming. It will be here before you know it. Food gets harder to find and the relentless cold fights you every day you're out in it. Look at your clothes. You'd never survive wearing what you have on."

Cori smiled. "It sounds like we need an expert. Someone who can help us make it through the winter."

"I'm not an expert. I've just lived in cold weather places all my life. I grew up in Michigan."

"Come with us. Eric needs other people after being alone for so long. So do you. And I need another girl to offset all the macho bullshit from the men."

Autumn smiled at that. "I like the idea of Eric having friends. He's been through so much."

"So have you. I think the last thing you two need is to be alone."

"I know you're right. Still, this is my home..."

"Think about it. We're not leaving until tomorrow. Whatever you decide, I'm good with it, but I'd love to have you with us. Eric too."

She nodded and grew silent again. A whistle rose up across the field, and Cori turned to see Dak waving an arm. He yelled.

"Dinner!"

She waved back and glanced once more at the fresh dirt of the grave. She knew in her heart that she would never return here and this was the last time she would stand over Flynn's grave.

"Thank you," she whispered and turned to go. Autumn

followed as a bird sang up high in the tree. Cori liked that sound. It felt like a good and peaceful sound.

The next morning they were up at first light, and after a quick breakfast, they picked up their gear and left the airfield behind. Cori watched her dad pause at the edge of the field and look back at the wreck of the TBM. If she were to guess, he would miss the plane. And the man that helped him fly it. Noah turned back and headed down the path to town.

Autumn and Eric were waiting, sitting on a bench in front of the old pharmacy, each of them sitting next to a pack that held all their worldly possessions. Autumn stood as they approached and Cori smiled.

"Watcha' gonna' do?" she asked but knew the answer even before Autumn spoke it.

"Can we come?"

"Of course."

Autumn hefted her pack to her back and helped Eric get his small backpack settled on his. She looked around at the town once more, nodded, and let Noah lead the way out of town. At the edge of town, Autumn looked back once, and sighed, then she turned and followed Cori and the rest toward North Dakota.

A new life was spread out before her and Cori knew in her heart that her new friend had found a family she could trust.

PART III

Malachi

13

M alachi shivered despite the layers of clothing he wore.

Inside the car that now served no purpose other than to shield him from the elements, the fever that raged through his body made him feel achy and cold. His stomach lurched, and he retched up yellow bile onto the floor of the passenger side. It was all he had left in his stomach. When he finished, he shivered again and felt his bowels twist into knots.

"Oh no, not again." He cursed and jumped from the car, wrestling with his pants as his bowels let loose. He squatted there in the snow, his body failing him.

The beaver he had killed four days ago had gone bad in his pack, and when he had eaten what was left the night before, the bacteria growing in its flesh had made him sick, and he cursed at himself for being such a fool. He had been hungry. And that had been a mistake.

He pulled his pants back up, glanced around, but then shook his head at himself. There was no one around. There was never anybody around. The world was a place he liked now. A place he could do as he pleased and there were no consequences. At least none that he found so far. He could be as cruel or nice as he pleased and the world only ignored him. At least what was left of the world.

He blew steam out of his mouth into the frigid air and pulled his coat tighter around him. The shivering became uncontrollable, and he slipped back into the stench of the car. He made a face to himself and sipped the water he had.

"Not too much," he mumbled to himself, "or you'll throw it back up."

Too late, his stomach revolted immediately, and he gave up the small amount of water and added it to the pool of bile on the floor of the car. He pounded his fist into the steering wheel in frustration.

He couldn't afford to be sick. He was finally close to his quarry, and he didn't want to lose track of her now.

"Stupid! Stupid! Stupid!"

The horn went off as his fist slipped and hit the center of the steering wheel. The battery was still good in this car, but he was out of gas. And nothing was in sight. No gas stations or even another car that he could siphon from. He was all alone on this desolate highway, the wind whipping the snow across the white surface and creating little eddies of frozen H_2O. On either side of the road, open fields stretched as far as the eye could see. Indiana—at least the northern part of it—was nothing but corn fields.

The shivering worsened, and the chattering of his teeth filled the empty car with a sound like the rustling of old bones. He wondered how long the ravages of the vile bacteria would keep hold of his body.

Movement caught his eye, and he looked up into the rearview mirror. He was surprised to see a human form moving in the road behind him. He watched in fascination—the fever forgotten—as the heavily cloaked form staggered in the wind and cold. This man—or woman—seemed to be in worse shape than him. As the shape grew closer, it was clear that this human was a woman. The gait of her steps, even as she shuffled and struggled, was that of a female and the long, black, hair that peaked out from beneath the knit cap suggested a woman. Still, he could be wrong. He'd been wrong along those lines before, and it had almost cost him his life.

The woman approached his car, and he could now hear the ice and snow crunching beneath her boots as she moved outside, oblivious to the automobile that sat dead in the middle of the road. At least until she staggered and fell against it. Then she stopped, looked up, and seemed confused. She reached out a hand and touched the cold metal of the car. Malachi held his breath.

The woman stood there, her face clouded over as the blue of her lips quivered in the cold starkness of her white face. Her hooded blue eyes seemed to take in nothing even as they looked over the object that she now realized sat in front of her. Then something passed for recognition in those cool, blue orbs and she pulled on the door handle of the car and opened the driver's door.

Shock filled her face for a brief instant, and then Malachi moved quick as a snake and struck her in the mouth with a fist as hard as a rock. Her blue eyes rolled up into her head, and she sagged to the ground next to the open door, blood now leaking from her split lip. Malachi chuckled and then started shivering again.

"Stupid bitch."

He got out of the car, and lifted her body up—she was light. Oh so light. He tossed her into the back seat where he climbed in beside her and arranged her unconscious form on the long bench seat of the old car. He pulled the knit cap off of her head and studied the pretty face.

"I bet your name is Roxy."

He smiled at the sound of the name. For some reason, he was sure that it was right. She looked like a Roxy.

She stirred, mumbled something incoherent, and then lay still again. He felt her face. She was burning up with a fever, just like him.

"You don't look so good, Roxy. I bet you'd be dead in an hour if I left you out there. You should thank me."

He chuckled again. He watched her for what seemed an eternity, wondering who she was. Why was she out here? Where was she going? Did she have a family? What did she do in her life before all things changed?

His eyes grew heavy as the fever burned incessantly inside him and without realizing what had happened, he fell asleep with her face in his dreams.

That was his first mistake.

14

Malachi fought upwards from the depth of his unconscious, the dream he seemed trapped in a nightmare he could not escape. He felt cold steel at his throat, and in the dream, the knife sliced through his skin like a razor, his own blood flowing hot and sticky down his chest. A scream formed on his lips, but no sound would escape.

When his eyes fluttered open and focused on his surroundings, an angry, but beautiful face hung over his. When he started to sit up, a voice came from the lips of the beautiful face. And it did not sound friendly. Not one bit.

"Move, and you die right now."

She spoke just above a whisper, and as the real world became more clear in his mind, he remembered her from before. The dried blood on her lower lip helped with the memory. The cold steel pressed to his neck from the dream was, in reality, not a vision. It was as real as any knife that he had seen.

"Hello." His voice sounded funny. Hollow. Like it was coming from the depths of an old oak barrel.

The blade at his throat pressed tighter to his skin.

"Who are you?" she whispered.

"Malachi."

"No. I don't give a shit about your name. Who are you?"

"I'm The Ratman."

"What does that mean?"

"It's what they call me."

"They?"

"The kids. Back in Florida. I eat rats. I.E. The Ratman."

Her eyelids tightened, and she breathed on his face, the smell of her, pleasant, considering the circumstances. She studied him for a few more seconds.

"You hit me."

"You fell."

"Bullshit. I remember. You didn't even wait for me to say a thing. You just reared back and slugged me with everything you had. I should kill you for that."

"You keep threatening me with death. Just do it, if you need to."

Her head tilted to the right, and she studied him again like an animal. He could see the wheels turning in her head and wondered if this was really it. Would he die like this in the cold at the hands of some beautiful woman?

"You look like a Ratman."

"Thanks."

She pulled away, lifted the blade from his throat, and sat back in the seat watching him closely. He sat up, rubbing his neck, and his hand came away with blood on his fingers. Not much, but enough to tell him he'd been that close to having his throat cut and his lifeblood spurt out all over the leather upholstery of the old car. He felt like fleeing but didn't know if he could get away from her in time. She looked lithe. Lithe and quick. Unlike her appearance from before when she had no idea where she was or who she was. This girl—this woman—was dangerous. Very dangerous.

"What's your name?" he asked.

"Roxy."

He couldn't believe it. He had been right. Of all the things…

She grinned and then laughed.

He realized she was mocking him. "For real? Your name is really Roxy?"

"Sure. Whatever. You already decided it for me, so it's Roxy."

"I decided?"

"Yeah. You were mumbling in your sleep about me and that I must be a Roxy."

She laughed again and then slipped the knife into some kind of sheath inside her coat. He didn't feel any relief at all at its disappearance. If he had to guess, she could have it out and at his throat again before he blinked.

"What's your real name?"

"Why does it matter?"

"I don't know. It just does."

She hesitated. "Adi."

"Adi."

"Yes," she answered in a breathy voice. "Adi Jordan."

"That's different."

She shrugged. "Not any different than The Ratman. Stupid."

"I didn't come up with it."

"But you like it."

"Why do you say that?"

"You call yourself the name. If you didn't like it, you wouldn't be telling people you're The Ratman."

"There are no people left."

"You told me."

"You asked."

She shook her head, reached for the door handle, and pulled on it. Nothing happened. She stared at him.

"Unlock the door."

He thumbed a button on his side, and the door locks popped up. She pulled the handle again, and the door opened, the cold air rushing in. She lifted herself up and out of the car in one smooth motion, and he marveled at how fit she was. He wondered what had been going on before that her body had failed her and she had been stumbling around in a numb fog.

He realized that his fever was gone and his stomach felt better. He was weak, but not ill. And that meant he would survive. At least a little longer.

She slammed the door behind her, and he watched as she moved off in the direction she had been going before, her dark form only a shape in the iced-over glass of the car. He rushed to open his door and climb out, the cold air hitting his skin like a slap in the face. The air smelled clean and fresh. Something he found odd that he would notice.

She moved away down the road, apparently done with him. For a bit, he was sure she would kill him, but for some reason, hadn't. And he wanted to know why.

He quickly grabbed his things from the front seat and hurried after her, leaving the car doors open. He jogged to catch up to her and settled in at her pace alongside her. She didn't acknowledge him for a moment. As he settled his pack onto his back, feeling a bit of energy return to him, she spoke.

"I travel alone."

"So do I."

She took a few more steps, and when he continued to pace her, she stopped and turned to him.

"I travel alone," she repeated, her hand twitching at her side. In his mind's eye, he could see that hand reach inside her coat, quick as lightning, and come out with that wicked knife held in its fingers.

"Look. You're going in that direction," he nodded his head toward the distant horizon, north, "I'm going in the same direction. If we end up walking side by side headed that way, who's to say we're traveling together? I walk here. You walk there. We're alone in our own space."

"You're an idiot." But she grinned in spite of herself. She turned and continued walking. He caught up again.

"What did you do? In your past life." He really wanted to know. It was bugging him, and he had a theory. Like the theory that her name was Roxy, which had been wrong.

"I killed people."

So much for his theory. "Like, the military?"

"Sort of."

"A spy?"

"Sort of."

"An assassin!"

She said nothing.

He thought about that for a few minutes—his and her boots crunching along in the snow and ice of the road—and the urge to flee in the opposite direction flooded back in. But he resisted. This woman fascinated him. She was like a drug. A drug that could make him feel euphoric and wonderful, or scared and on the edge of death. And right now he was feeling euphoric that she had not killed him back in the car. If he had been in her situation—a victim of some rogue stranger's violence—he would have killed that person without hesitation.

"I've killed people," he said. Walking next to her the words sounded lame. Like some teenager trying to impress a girl.

When he looked over at her, she was grinning, but she didn't say anything.

"So, how many people have you killed?"

"Too many."

"You sound like you regret it."

"I do."

"Then why did you do it?"

She didn't answer for a second. "Why did you do it?"

"Because it felt good." Malachi realized that it had. He had answered without thinking about it. He had enjoyed the act and would do it again. Even if he didn't have to.

She frowned, studied him for a moment, and then looked away. "It never feels good."

"Then why do it?"

"It was my job."

"So, you're saying you never killed just because. You never killed for fun?"

"No."

"Ever?"

He could see her thinking about it, and he smiled. Maybe she was like him after all. He could like this girl. Really like her. He even entertained the idea that he could love her and that was really out of character for him. He hadn't felt this way with Michalla. He pretended he did because he wanted an heir. A son. But he didn't love Michalla or even like her. More of an obsession. Yes. That was a better word for his relationship with Michalla. Obsession.

"What kind of name is Adi, anyway?"

"What kind of name is Malachi?"

"No, really. I've never heard it before."

"Israeli."

"Mossad?"

She nodded.

"How did you end up in the U.S.?"

"Why all these questions? I'm not really into the whole, 'this is my life' thing."

"You're different. Different than anybody else around here."

"That's not saying much. There's nobody left."

"True. Still. It's been a long time since I had a conversation with somebody like me."

"I'm not like you."

"How do you know?"

"I just do. I'm not like you. Trust me on that."

"I think you're going to find that you are."

"I'm not going to spend enough time with you to find out. At the next town, you go your way, and I'll go mine."

"What if that way is in the same direction?"

"It won't be."

"Where are you going?"

She turned and looked down the road. "That way."

"Me too. For what purpose?"

"I'm searching for someone."

"Me too. See? Who are you looking for?"

"My daughter."

"I'm looking for the mother of my child. My son. Can't get any more similar than that."

She grew silent again, and they walked without talking for a few minutes. He kept looking over at her. Her jet-black hair was so dark he was sure it was dyed. But who would dye their hair in this world now as it was? Her nose was small and almost perfect, her lips now red and full, unlike the blue from before. When she felt him staring, she turned, and her eyes narrowed. But, oh. Those eyes. They were the most intense blue he'd ever seen, and he couldn't seem to look away. She had a small mole on her left cheek. A beauty mark. And on her it was beautiful. It gave her an exotic look, and he could see the middle eastern bloodlines in the shape of her face and set of her mouth.

"Stop it," she said.

"What?"

"You're leering. Just stop. I'm not some chick you're going to bang because we're the 'only two people left on earth.' I'm not going to fall for you while we walk down this cold, barren, road in the middle of nowhere U.S.A. I'm not in need of companionship or a lover, nor am I in need of someone to look after me. I'm perfectly capable of taking care of myself and prefer it that way."

"I'm not leering."

"You were."

"Was not."

She shook her head. "I could have killed you easily back there. But I didn't. That doesn't mean you owe me. It only means I wasn't in the mood."

"I could have killed you as well."

"No, you couldn't. I wouldn't let you."

"You were in pretty bad shape. I knocked you out with one hit. I could have easily put a bullet in your head right then and there, but I didn't. That makes us even."

Her hand moved with incredible speed, and he watched in fascination as the blade came out again and was pressed to his throat before he even realized what had happened. He froze. She moved her face close to his, and he could smell her skin. He felt himself becoming aroused, and he wondered if he'd die that way. *Not a bad way to go*, he thought.

"I can still kill you," she whispered. "Do you want to push me? I would suggest otherwise."

"Dying at your hand would be...pleasurable."

She tilted her head again as she had done in the car. A grin slowly formed on her lips. "You're a psycho."

"I am."

She slowly pulled the knife away and slipped it back into her coat. She took a deep breath, appeared more relaxed, and moved away. He watched her back for a few seconds and then caught up to her.

"I like you," he said.

"Yeah? Get in line."

He laughed, waving his arms at the empty, wide-open space, and when he looked back at her, she was smiling again. Yes. He could like this girl. Like her a lot.

15

For the next two days, they walked.

And Malachi felt as if he were in heaven. If he actually believed in such a thing. She became more relaxed and open with him as they talked and tried to keep warm. He learned her daughter's name was Joelle. Jo. And he told her he wanted to name his son Malachi too. She grunted but didn't seem to care.

The road stretched on and on, its straight plunge into the distant horizon an almost impossible feat of physics. At least to Malachi's eyes. It seemed as if the road would never turn or climb or descend or end. The unending empty corn fields filled their vision from east to west as the road led ever northward. Always north.

On that first night, they got lucky and found an old farmhouse, the long-dead occupants nothing but desiccated skeletons lying next to each other in the yard, a shotgun in the bony hands of one of them. Malachi couldn't figure out why they had decided to end their lives out here in the overgrown weeds of the farm. Maybe they had some weird connection with the earth. Who knew?

It was good to be out of the cold and wind, and as Malachi started a fire in the fireplace, Adi searched the kitchen and found a few unopened cans of beans and corn. Malachi really wanted some meat, but beggars could not be choosers in this world.

They ate the beans and corn from paper plates with plastic forks and drank a bottle of wine from plastic cups. The wine was especially good, and it made him forget that a couple of days before he'd been puking his guts out, thoughts of his life coming to an end all but a distant memory.

She had shed her coat, and a few more layers of clothes as the house warmed, and he could not help but notice that she had a body to kill for. She seemed to enjoy the way he followed her movements with his eyes, trying his best not to stare, but not being able to help it. She said nothing about his 'leering' again, but she didn't hide the fact that she noticed it. In fact, she seemed to tease him with the way she moved. And that was just fine with him.

They slept on the floor in front of the fire, the soft glowing light casting shadows across everything, her beauty more pronounced in the flattering warmth and that golden glow. Just before he fell asleep, he found her staring at him with those eyes. He wondered what she was thinking, her gaze steady and serene. She finally turned away, and he fell asleep with those eyes in his dreams.

In the morning, they ate the leftover beans and corn and headed out again, leaving the farmhouse to the dead owners and the cold wind. They marched north, the never-ending road seeming to laugh at their feeble progress. It was as if it were saying to him, "I'm just an illusion. Like a hamster wheel. I never end, and I just keep circling around."

That night, they were not as lucky with shelter. Nothing was in sight as the sun set and the temperatures plummeted. They were forced to build a fire next to a bush on the side of the road and huddle near it. And they had nothing to eat. They melted snow on the fire and drank the hot liquid to give them something in their bellies. It did little to satisfy Malachi's rumbling stomach.

The wind died down with the setting of the sun, and though it was cold, at least it was still. Malachi lay on one side of the fire, its warmth barely keeping the cold away. He shivered occasionally and felt miserable. He sat up, looked over the glow of the fire at Adi, and saw her lip quivering. Her eyes were closed, but he knew her to be awake. She looked miserable. He got up, went over to her, and lay down behind her wrapping his arms around her and pressing his body against hers. She stiffened, turned, and started hitting him in the chest.

"Get away!"

"You're freezing," he argued. "We need to keep each other warm."

"Bull. You have only one thing on your mind."

"Yeah. Keeping warm."

He pulled her closer, and she fought him again for a moment, but he could tell she really wasn't trying. She finally stopped, made a sound in her throat, and lay still. He squirmed tighter to her, and he felt her start to protest again, but changed her mind and relented. After a minute, he felt her body relax into him and her shivering cease.

"Better?"

"I'm sure it is for you," she said. "I don't like being this close to you."

"Suck it up."

She was silent for a few seconds, then she laughed, and the sound made him feel better. Such a good thing when she laughed. He'd never thought he'd like it so much. He pressed his face into the warmth of her hair and let her scent fill his senses. He closed his eyes and was soon asleep.

The next morning, he woke alone and sat up. She was

nowhere in sight, and he felt a pang of panic at the thought that she was gone. He stood, turned in a full circle, and could see nothing but empty space in all directions.

"Adi!" he shouted, his voice carrying across the expanse.

If she were gone, she couldn't be that far ahead. He packed his things in his backpack as fast as he could and took off at a run, north. He slowed to a jog after a few minutes, searching the horizon for any sign of her.

After half an hour, he saw her, head down, pressing forward along the empty, cold road. He picked up his pace, and when he caught up to her, she wouldn't even look his way.

Catching his breath, keeping pace with her, he kept looking her way. Finally, he said, "Why?"

"Why what?"

"Why did you leave me?"

"I told you. I travel alone."

"You're pissed because you had to sleep next to me. That's it, isn't it? It kept you warm, didn't it?"

She said nothing, staring at the road in front of her, putting one foot in front of the other.

"Hey. Look at me." He reached out and grabbed her arm.

She moved with that lightning speed of hers, the hand inside the coat and her other arm pushing him away. Only this time, the hand came out with a pistol pointed at his midsection. Her face betrayed the anger that appeared without warning.

"Don't touch me!"

"All right. I won't." He raised his hands and stopped walking.

"Don't ever touch me. You don't have the right to touch me."

"You're right. My bad."

"Go."

"Adi..."

"I said, go. Back where you came from. I don't need you with me."

"You're just saying that because..."

She loaded a round in the chamber and pointed the gun at his head. It never wavered in her hand.

"You have five seconds to turn around and start walking."

"Adi. Let me..."

"Four...three..."

He stared into her eyes for the count of two, saw that she meant it, and turned around. He took a step away from her as she stopped counting. He stood there with his hands up in the air and his back to her.

"You could have killed me before," he said, "but you didn't."

"Just go," she said, her voice hoarse and raw.

He wanted to turn and plead with her, but he knew it would be a mistake. He took a step. Then another. And another. And lowered his hands. He walked away back the way he came and never heard her move. He walked for what seemed like only a few minutes and then turned around.

She was gone.

MALACHI SPENT the whole day in an old barn, the anger at her leaving second only to the sadness that he felt with her gone. He didn't like how that felt. Couldn't understand what was going on with him. He'd never felt this way before and decided he would never feel this way again.

He built a small fire in the middle of the barn, caught a few rats, and ate them after cooking them until they were burnt and crunchy. He didn't want to repeat the stomach issues from a few days ago.

He slept in the barn and the next morning, he hefted his things and headed north again. He was sure that Adi would be long gone by now.

"Good riddance," he mumbled to no one. "Time to find Michalla."

He walked and walked, the endless road stretching out to infinity. A few more farmhouses dotted the land, and that meant he must be getting closer to a town. Sure enough, a sign appeared sticking up out of the snow, informing all who traveled this road that "Christmas Town" was two miles ahead.

"What a stupid name for a town. Let me guess. All the shops only sell things for Christmas. Can't wait."

He marched on, noting after another half mile that he could see smoke in the distance. His heart took a small gallop in his chest as the first thing he thought was that Adi was there. But she wouldn't have stopped. She would be long gone from any town. Especially if it had people in it.

As the first buildings of the small town came into sight, snow started to fall. It was getting darker, and the temperature started to fall. He shivered in his coat and cursed the small flakes as they tumbled out of the darkening sky. He would have to stay in the town for the night to escape the bitter cold that he knew would soon fill his world.

He walked into town, its dark windows following him as he strode down the center of the main street. A few decorations hung from the lamp post, their tattered remains flapping in the light breeze, the once bright colors faded and lost. Of course, they were Christmas decorations, just as he imagined.

A few store signs still hung in the shops, proclaiming "20% off!" "Sale!!" "Get your Christmas ornaments before the season!" One store sold ammo and guns, its sign claiming "the best prices in all of the state." He wandered over and peered inside the window. The shelves were empty.

So far, he'd seen no one. The town looked deserted and cold, but he was sure he could find a place to settle in for the night. He might even be able to catch a rat or two for dinner.

He turned back to Main Street and continued along its

lonely route. A few cars sat rotting in the street, their engines cold and dead, the paint fading and dirty. Inside one of them, a skeleton sat behind the wheel, its hands locked in a death grip that would never let go. Malachi wondered why the occupant died that way. The more he thought about any logical answer, the more bizarre his imagination became. He shook his head at his own thoughts and stopped in the middle of the street, pausing at a sound.

Was that music?

He turned his head and heard it again. Yes, it was. Coming from up ahead. He moved toward the end of town, and the music grew louder. At the end of the street, a bar sat on the west side. From the other side of the windows, yellow light glowed, and the origin of the music emanated from the other side of its door. He could hear voices now as well. Humans. The door opened, the music grew louder, and a male voice shouted as a man stumbled from within the bar. He leaned up against a support for the porch roof, bent over, and vomited into the street. He wiped his mouth and then stumbled back inside.

Malachi watched all this with a kind of detached fascination. He despised people. Avoided them if he could. But it looked warm inside the bar. And it had been a long time since he'd had a drink. Maybe they would have food. He wrestled with whether or not to enter, then his stomach won over as it growled loudly in the street.

"Fine. I'll go."

He walked to the door, opened it, and was greeted with the warm smell of roasting meat and cigarette smoke. The place was hopping. About ten men were scattered around the room, and they all turned to see who had opened the door. The conversations they were engaged in stopped, and the lone man playing guitar paused and stared. The silence dragged out for a few seconds until one man scolded Malachi.

"Close the door. The cold is getting in."

Malachi stepped into the bar, letting the door close behind him. The men turned back to their conversations, and the guitar man resumed his song. Malachi walked up to the bar, and a scraggly skinny kid of about twenty limped over slinging a dirty rag over his shoulder. He looked Malachi up and down, and then kind of chuckled to himself. Malachi disliked him immediately.

"Money's no good here," the kid said. "We have whiskey and wine. No beer."

"How do I pay for it?"

"Bullets. A shot for a shot."

Malachi felt torn. Ammo was a precious thing. He had some in his pack, but was it worth the whiskey? He decided he'd have just one. He rummaged around in his pack and set a single bullet on the bar. The skinny kid snatched it up, and it disappeared inside his pocket.

"What'll it be?"

"Whiskey."

The kid grinned and set a single shot glass on the bar in front of Malachi, reached beneath the bar, and brought out a plain glass bottle. He poured a brown liquid into the glass. He put the bottle back and moved away. Malachi picked up the shot glass and took a sip. It was whiskey all right, and it felt good going down. He licked his lips and yelled at the kid.

"Got a sec?"

The kid walked back over, looked him up and down again and waited.

"I haven't eaten in a while."

"We've got venison stew on the stove."

"How much?"

"Two shots for a bowl. Extra shot if you want bread and butter with it."

Malachi tossed three bullets onto the bar. "All of it."

"Sure thing, Mister."

He turned to get the stew, but Malachi stopped him. "Seen girl in here? Dark hair. Pretty. Would have been yesterday or so."

The kid eyed him. "No."

"You wouldn't have been able to miss her."

"No. No girl."

Malachi nodded, and the kid walked away. He came back a few minutes later with a steaming bowl of stew and a big hunk of buttered bread. It smelled fantastic, and Malachi dug in. The meat was tough and stringy, but it tasted good. He ate it all and then worked on the bread. At least he wouldn't have to hunt rats tonight.

A man in a big leather coat sat down next to Malachi and turned to him. He grinned at him but said nothing. Malachi tried to ignore him, but the man just kept staring, that stupid grin on his face. Finally, Malachi turned to him.

"Need something, Mister?"

"Nope. Just trying to figure where you're from. Not here, that's for sure. I'd bet down south. Georgia?"

"Florida."

The man slapped the bar with a big dirty hand. "I knew it." He turned and shouted at another man sitting at a table a few feet away. "I told you! He says, Florida."

The other man nodded but didn't move.

"Got a name, my friend."

"Malachi."

The man laughed. "Give that to me again."

"Malachi." He punctuated every syllable slowly.

"Weird name. But hey, I don't judge."

"Right."

Malachi sipped his whiskey and wished the big man would go away. He didn't feel like talking. In fact, all he wanted to do was sleep now that his belly was full and the whiskey was starting to relax him. He decided to have one more, and then o hole up for the night. He called the skinny

, more, just like before." He set a bullet onto the bar.

Sure thing." The kid poured him another shot and then went back over to his conversation at the other end of the bar.

Leather Coat was still staring at him.

"Where ya headed?" the man asked.

"Why do you care?"

"Hey, just trying to make conversation."

"I like to drink alone if you don't mind."

"Sure. Sure. I'll let you be."

He slipped from the barstool and moved over to his buddy at the table. He sat and said something to the other man, who chuckled, looking Malachi's way. Something bugged Malachi about the two of them, and it made him antsy. If it had been just the three of them and not a whole room full of these backwoods idiots, he'd probably have killed them by now. He turned back to his drink and sipped the whiskey.

A door opened at the back of the bar, and the sound of cursing rose above the music. Malachi watched as a man emerged from the room, his lip bloody and the fingers of his right hand bent at a weird angle. He looked furious and cursed again. Malachi couldn't make out what he was saying, but he started arguing with the man in the leather coat. It got more heated, and Leather Coat finally stood and punched the bleeding man in the face. He went down to his knees. The room grew quiet for a few seconds, and then everybody went back to their business.

It was then that Malachi realized why those two men bothered him. Leather Coat's buddy wore a cap. A knitted cap. The same knitted cap that belonged to Adi.

Malachi's hand froze in mid-sip as the door opened in the back again—another man entering—and he caught a quick glimpse of someone else inside. Sitting in a chair. A female. Dark hair. And blood. Blood on her face.

He found himself moving before he realized his brain had told him to move.

The conversations and music grew quieter as a roaring filled his ears. Someone shouted his name, but he didn't hear the rest. As he reached for the door handle at the back of the room, a shot rang out, and something whacked into the wood frame of the door just to the right of Malachi's head. He hardly noticed.

He flung the door open and looked into Adi's angry eyes. Then recognition filled them with a kind of hope and exhilaration.

She sat in a wooden chair, her hands tied behind her, blood leaking from her nose and lips. Her top was ripped, with one breast exposed. The man who had entered stood in front of her, his hands loosening his trousers as he turned to see who was disturbing his fun. Malachi punched him in the face, and he went down. Another gunshot rang out as he stepped to Adi.

"Cut me loose," she said, calmly.

He pulled his knife and did as she asked. Malachi felt someone behind him as Adi's eyes moved. She grabbed the knife from him before he could even think about moving and watched in fascination as she moved with the speed of a cheetah. Her arm arced over his head and he heard a weird sound behind him as something warm and wet splashed on his neck. When he turned, Leather Coat had a hand to his throat as he sagged to his knees, blood spurting from his cut carotid artery.

Leather Coat's buddy burst into the room, and Adi stepped gracefully to him, her knife hand swinging in an arc from her hip upwards into his belly just below his rib cage. He said one word.

"Argh!"

Just like in the cartoons that Malachi used to watch as a kid.

"Argh." Adi thrust upward with the knife, and he sagged to the ground as she pulled it free of his body. More blood mixed with the blood of Leather Coat. She turned to Malachi.

"Gun." She stretched out her hand.

Malachi pulled his pistol from his coat and placed it in her hand. She slipped the bloody knife into her waistband, loaded the gun, and moved into the main bar area as the rest of the men began to realize what was happening. She opened fire and killed the closest five men as fast as the gun would fire in her hands. Her skill with the weapon was amazing, each bullet finding its mark at the center of her victim's forehead.

A man at the bar was pulling out a big revolver, but he was way too slow to do any harm as Adi fired again and struck him in the throat. He dropped the big revolver and grabbed at his ruined neck, a wet gurgling coming from his mouth as he collapsed in a heap. Two men ran for the door, but she cut them down before they could make it and they fell onto each other blocking the way out. She turned, found another man trying to flee, and shot him in the back of the head. He was dead before he hit the ground.

The skinny kid behind the bar was the only man left standing, and she pointed the weapon at him as he raised his hands.

"I've got no beef with you, lady. I'm just the bartender."

"You watched," she said and pulled the trigger.

His face exploded, and Malachi stared as the skinny kid's hands trembled with spasms, his brain trying to send signals along damaged and ruined nerve endings. He stood for a second, his whole body quivering, then it gave out, and he fell behind the bar. Silence filled the room.

She lowered the gun, checked its load, and then moved over to where Malachi stood in the doorway. She handed the weapon back to him.

"It's empty."

16

Malachi poured whiskey onto the bullet wound. He expected it to make a sizzling sound, but, of course, it didn't. Adi made a small noise in her throat and flinched, but that was all.

The bullet had gone in and out of the flesh of her upper arm sometime during The Christmas Town Massacre (as Malachi liked to call it). She hadn't even noticed until it was all over and Malachi had pointed to the blood running down her arm. She had only shrugged.

"I can't feel it," she had said.

But he was sure she was feeling it now. Only she didn't show it.

He wrapped the wound in an old t-shirt he'd found in the house. It had looked clean and washed. She watched him work and when he looked into her eyes something had changed. She stared into his with a different look. When he finished, she rubbed it with her other hand and said, "Thank you."

"You'd do the same for me."

"Maybe." She grinned, and he shook his head.

"I'm curious," he said.

"About what?"

"How did you let them catch you off guard? I mean, you're like a ninja. There's no way those men should have been able to tie you up and hold you hostage."

"I fell asleep. When I woke, a gun was pointed at my face."

"Hmm. You didn't hear them?"

"No. I was tired."

"You need someone to help keep you alert and safe."

"I do."

He busied himself with cleaning up the blood and shirts. When he went to stand, she reached out her hand and grabbed his arm to stop him.

"If you hadn't come along..."

"It's okay. I did. That's all that matters."

She pursed her lips and closed her eyes. "If you hadn't saved me, I'd have gone through hell and been dead after they were through with me. I owe you."

"You would have found a way."

"Believe me; I wouldn't have."

He shrugged. "I'll be gone in the morning. You'll be fine. Just keep it clean."

"Malachi. I made a mistake. Stay. Stay with me. I need you."

He found her eyes and held them. She was sincere. He could see it. And something else. Gratitude. He liked that coming from her. It made him feel...powerful. She made him better. And she was a badass. A total badass.

"You won't try and kill me in my sleep?"

She grinned and shook her head, no.

"You won't leave me in the early hours of the morning, me, wondering where the hell you have gone?"

She shook her head, no.

"I saw your breast."

She tilted her head the way he liked, and the smile changed. He liked that smile.

"So?"

"So?"

"What did you think?"

"Of your breast?"

She nodded.

He pretended to consider it. She continued to smile at him. "I was kind of busy at the time, so I didn't really pay attention."

"Bull."

He laughed. "All right. If you hadn't been tied to a chair, I probably would have leered at you in lust."

"Who knows? You might get to see the other one too."

She stood, touched his arm with her fingertips, and moved away. "I'm exhausted," she said. "I'm going to hit the sack. See you in the morning."

"You better be here."

"I will."

She smiled once more at him and then moved down the hall and into an empty room. He sat back on the couch and watched the fire. He was asleep before he even realized he was tired.

In the middle of the night, Malachi sat up. Something wasn't right. He looked around the dark room and found Adi standing at the window, her curvy figure silhouetted by the moonlight streaming in. He went to her.

"Pack your stuff and get dressed," she said. "We're leaving."

She turned and went to her room to gather her things. Malachi saw movement out on the street and watched as two men on horseback dismounted and went into the house across the street.

They were looking for something. Or someone.

He packed his things and put on his gear. She stood waiting by the stairs, and when he was ready, she led the way down. They slipped out the back door into the cold night, and she moved off to the north through the overgrown yard. He followed. The men on horseback did not.

They moved under cover of the houses and woods for about an hour and when she felt better about it, emerged onto the road where the going was easier. They walked for another hour and then she pointed to a small copse of trees.

"I'm tired. Let's stop here for the rest of the night."

They wouldn't build a fire for fear of it being seen by the searching men, so they huddled next to each other, the cold seeping into his clothes. She squirmed next to him, and he wrapped his arm around her, her arms slipping inside of his coat. The one blanket he had in his pack he wrapped around them. They kept each other warm for the rest of the night, sleeping fitfully in the cold.

Malachi woke to the sun shining in his eyes and her warm body missing. He looked around but didn't see her. He shook his head, feeling foolish that he had believed her. She had left him again. He stood, cursing himself and folding his blanket, the feel of her softness next to him a fresh memory. He bent to put the blanket back in his pack, and she spoke from behind him.

"Ready?"

He spun around, finding her standing there with one hand on her hip and one eyebrow raised. She smiled.

"I thought you left again," he said.

"I had to pee."

"You had to pee."

"I had to pee," she repeated.

She moved to her things and bundled them up. She shoved them into his pack since she didn't have one. He watched her in silence. She moved to him and touched his face with surprisingly warm fingers.

"I told you I wouldn't leave."

She moved away and started walking down the road. He

caught up to her and kept pace, feeling his face tighten as the grin on his lips spread. He watched her black hair shift in the breeze, her skin white in the light of the new day, and her lips dark red.

"Stop staring at me." But she grinned and looked sideways at him.

He did as he was told and they walked on, leaving Christmas Town behind.

THEY TREKKED north along the never-ending highway, the white ribbon of snow-covered road now bending around rivers and lakes and climbing and descending gentle hills. The change in the landscape went mostly unnoticed by Malachi, his attention only on the woman next to him.

She seemed unusually open and chatty since the massacre at Christmas Town. They talked for hours about their past and what lay ahead.

At one point she asked him about Michalla and his unborn son.

"Who is she to you? I mean, if she's carrying your son, she must be important to you."

Malachi paused, wanting to make sure he got it right. If she knew the truth, she would turn around and leave him standing in the cold.

"She was a mistake. I mean, the relationship. Our son, I like to think was meant to be. When she left me, I was angry. What right did she have to take my son from me? I went after her and eventually found her, only to lose her again when the military took her away."

"What do you mean, took her away?"

"She had become involved with two teenagers and another man. They came across a town in south Florida on their trek to

Miami, and a doctor in the town basically used them as guinea pigs. I'm not sure exactly what happened—I wasn't there—but when I arrived, helicopters were whisking them away to a base further north. Later I learned from the townspeople that the base they took her to was Fort Bragg."

"So you went after her."

He nodded. "When I got to the base, she had disappeared. I 'persuaded' a soldier to tell me where they had gone."

"North Dakota."

"Right. Minot Air Force Base."

She nodded, seeming to buy into the story. It wasn't all a lie. The part about where they had taken her and the town in south Florida was all correct. His persuasion of the soldier had involved torture and death, but she didn't need to know that little fact.

"Sometimes I'm amazed by life's coincidences," he said. "I mean, here I am, searching for my unborn son and his mother, sick on the road in the middle of nowhere and you stumble into my life headed to the same place."

"I don't believe in coincidence," she said. "The fact that my daughter was stationed at Minot Air Force Base and I'm on my way to see if she survived has nothing to do with you or anybody else."

"Are you sure about that?"

"Positive."

"What if I hadn't found you tied up in that bar? What then?"

"I'd be dead."

"Right."

She seemed to ponder the fact but didn't say anything again for a long time; when she did, she changed the subject completely.

"Do you know how to cook lasagna?"

"What?" He looked at her like she'd gone crazy.

"I want lasagna."

"We're lucky if we get rabbit. Or rat."

"Do you know how to cook it?"

"Sure. It's easy if you have the right stuff."

"The next town. We're gonna find the right stuff."

"We don't have ground beef. And probably won't find it in the next town, or any town for that matter. I haven't seen a cow in ages."

"Right there." She pointed.

He'd been too busy talking to her to notice, but standing at the edge of the fence along the road was a cow. It stared at them chewing the little grass it could find poking up out of the snow. The steam escaping its nostrils proved to him that it was not an illusion.

"You've got to be kidding me," he mumbled.

Adi walked over to it and stuck her hand through the bob wire fence. She rubbed the cow's head, and it took a step away but did not move off. Malachi searched the field it was in and found a farmhouse off in the distance. Smoke rose from its chimney. He pointed.

"It has an owner."

Adi followed his finger and frowned at the sight. "Maybe they're willing to share their cow."

"I doubt it."

"Let's find out."

"What if they're armed?"

"Oh. I'm sure they are. But so are we." She smiled and climbed over the fence.

He watched her walk toward the house, and he shook his head. He climbed over the fence—a feat that actually ended up being harder than she made it look—and caught up with her.

"I hope you know what you're doing," he said.

She just smiled.

The house was large. A two-story affair with brick construction and ivy growing up the outside on the south wall. The fireplace was active with a trail of gray smoke drifting off with the small breeze. Another cow scavenged along the edge of the fence near the drive. It looked up at them as they approached but made no sound. She led the way up to the side of the house by a window and peered inside. Malachi did the same from the other side.

The house at first seemed empty, then a man's shadow moved into the room and sat on what must be a couch. They both pulled back from the window.

"What now?" he asked.

"Let's do this the old fashion way," she said.

"How's that?"

"We knock."

She smiled and made her way to the front door. He followed, and when they were both standing on the porch, she reached up her hand and rapped it on the big door. A dog barked. Weird. This was all too normal to be real.

The door opened, and Malachi's mouth fell open as the woman standing at the door greeted them with a smile and an M4 rifle in her hands. Her hair, her eyes, her lips, her nose, the shape of her face, and the move of her body were all familiar to Malachi, so much so that he couldn't speak for a second.

"Can I help you?" the woman asked.

Adi was about to say something when Malachi spoke first.

"Hello, Michalla."

The woman frowned.

17

The sight of Michalla standing directly in front of him brought a wave of emotions and feelings so strong that Malachi had a hard time containing himself. Adi had turned to him and was staring at him, her mouth set in a small smile, her eyes wide and just as surprised as his must be. He looked Michalla up and down and noticed something wasn't right. She should be months pregnant by now and showing. Nothing. Something must have gone wrong with the pregnancy, and he became agitated. She noticed immediately and adjusted the M4 in her hands. The dog they had heard barking appeared next to her and growled at them.

"Skitch, no," she said.

"I won't hurt you, Michalla," Malachi said.

"I'm not Michalla. I'm Cori. I'm her sister. How do you know Michalla and where do you know her from?"

This Cori woman became very excited, and as the information filtered through Malachi's head, it fell into place in all the right circles and openings and made sense. This was the sister Michalla had been searching for. The almost twin sister who looked remarkably like her. But now that he studied her more closely he could see some subtle differences. But oh, they were subtle. The set of her eyes was a little wider than Michalla's. Her mouth curved down in one corner, whereas Michalla's was perfect when she smiled. A little beauty mark sat next to her nose, its presence clearly different from Michalla's face.

The dog continued to growl in protest, and a man appeared behind Cori. He carried an M4 as well and looked much more concerned about their visitors than Cori, who took a step outside toward Malachi and Adi. Adi took a step backward and pressed herself against Malachi.

"I'm so sorry," Malachi said. "You look so much like her. I immediately thought it was her. Of course, you're her sister. How could you not be? She talked so much about you."

Cori's face lit up. She turned to the man behind her and smiled then turned back.

"Quiet Skitch," she scolded the dog and rubbed his head, and the dog settled a bit, but still looked very dangerous. "You've seen Michalla? You know her? Where? Where is she? How do you know her?"

A flood of questions was flung at Malachi, and he tried to open his mouth to answer, but more questions stopped him. He smiled at Cori, knowing full well that what he would tell her would be mostly lies. But it would make her feel better.

"I met her in Florida. She was looking for you, as a matter of fact. On her way to Miami."

Cori nodded. "Yes. Was she well? Did she look good?"

"Yes. She looked great."

"How did you meet her?"

"I was living in the big amusement park, and she came through it one day. She stayed with me for about a week, and I fed her and let her rest up. She was pretty exhausted at the time and starving. She told me all about her family."

Adi watched this back and forth with amusement but didn't say a word.

"I'm being rude," Cori said. She turned to the man behind her. "We have enough for them, don't we Dak?"

"We don't know them," the man said.

"If Michalla trusted them, we can too."

Dak studied Malachi and Adi and nodded. "Sure. We have enough. We have a whole cow. Might as well make use of it."

Cori stepped back and opened the door wider. "Come on in. What were your names?"

"Malachi and Adi."

"Hi. Come on in and meet everybody."

She led the way into the house, and Malachi let Adi follow her in first. The dog moved to Dak's side and stayed close to him, and Malachi realized it must be the man's pet. Or maybe even more. The dog seemed very well trained. Hopefully, it wouldn't be a problem. Most animals, especially dogs, did not like Malachi.

In the main room, a few more people sat on comfortable-looking furniture. They were introduced all around, and Malachi did his best to remember their names. The Autumn woman was easy as her hair matched her name and the little dark-haired boy must be her son.

"Dad, this is Malachi and Adi. They know Michalla. They've actually seen her and spent time with her in Florida."

Adi finally spoke. "You're the astronaut. Col. Noah Dresdon." She went to shake his hand. "Big fan."

Noah laughed and seemed to buy into this whole charade that Malachi and Adi were putting on. Malachi was glad that Adi was going along with things. That they were working as a team. She kept giving him looks but didn't contradict anything he said.

The conversation about Michalla continued into dinner, and as Malachi dug himself ever deeper into stories and lies about Michalla, the others never seemed to question or disbelieve what he told them. In fact, they were overwhelmingly happy to have them in this house that they temporarily called home.

Later, when Malachi and Adi were in the room that the others so graciously offered them, Adi questioned his tactics.

"You do know that when her father sees her for the first time, months pregnant and fat, she'll tell him all about you two."

Malachi, in fact, did know. In his mind, Noah would be dead before they reached Minot Air Force Base, and maybe even Cori and Dak as well. Yes, they would all have to die. All of them except Adi. Adi would live and be with him forever. Of that he was certain.

PART IV

Christa

18

Christa Flaherty tightened the billet on the saddle and mounted her horse, Lightning.

He tossed his head once and made a noise with his lips, the steam escaping from his nostrils making her feel cold despite the layers of clothing she wore beneath the expensive arctic coat. She adjusted her gloves and snickered at Lightning, tapping her heels into his flanks. He trotted for a few steps and then settled into a good pace. She could sense that he wanted to get moving.

The temperature hovered around the zero mark. She didn't have a thermometer but her years in this part of North Dakota made her acutely aware of what the world was doing around her. She loved being outdoors. Especially in the winter. The crisp air and clear skies made her feel one with the earth. Kind of a cliché, she knew, but it was really how she felt. Especially now that she was all alone.

The foot of snow that had fallen two days before still looked clean and new, the brightness something that hurt her eyes. She slipped on the sunglasses that had belonged to her dad. He had been an air force aviator stationed at Minot, and the glasses were considered old by many, but to her, they did their job well and let her carry a part of her father with her. Sometimes, she could even smell his scent on them. Or at least what she remembered he smelled like.

She reigned in Lightning at the top of the rise and looked out over the pasture below. Her pasture. Or at least what once had been her family's homestead. The ranch house where she'd grown up sat at the very back of the land right up against the edge of the big forest. Smoke curled from the chimney, evidence that the men who had stolen it from her were still inside. Five of them. All brothers. Kids that had grown up in the town and gone to school with her. And now were the trash of the county. At least what was left of the county.

The Roscoe brothers were trouble. Had been for years. And before all the sadness and death of the plague, Christa's job as sheriff had been to put those boys in their place from time to time. And that had pissed them off. Pissed them off good. So, when the world had come to an end, they decided to pay 'ol sheriff Christa Flaherty a visit on her ranch and steal it out from underneath her.

Today, she would take it back from them.

Or die trying.

The M4A1 rifle that sat strapped to her chest felt good. It had been a long time since she'd had one and she'd owed Tyler up at Minot a couple of bottles of good whiskey for letting her take it. Tyler had been one of her staff when she'd been an M.P. at the air force base back in the day. The trip to the now almost deserted base had taken the better part of yesterday but had been well worth the time. She was saddened to see it in disarray and neglected, but most of the world was that way now. Tyler had survived the pandemic and was now part of the skeleton crew that had remained at Minot doing their best to keep it up. The rest of the soldiers and staff had moved to The ARK up in the hills.

She had trotted right in through the abandoned main gate, made her way through the ghost town of the main street, and tied Lightning up to a lamppost next to the M.P. office. She had walked in and found Tyler asleep with his feet up on the desk. She had cleared her throat, and he about fell off his chair.

"Christa! You're alive. I somehow knew you'd survive." He grinned at her, starting to salute, then remembered she was no longer in the service and put his hand down.

"Hello, Tyler. Where is everybody?"

"I'm just about it. A couple more over at logistics and the Colonel in his office but everybody else is up at The ARK."

She had felt sadness fill her at the huge loss of life that had taken place. She missed her family and friends. She missed the way the world had been.

They chatted about old times and people who had died and finally Christa told Tyler why she was there.

"I need weapons."

"Weapons we have," Tyler said. "What do you want?"

She told him, and he grinned. "I'm not supposed to do this, but for you, anything. You just bring me some good whiskey, and we'll call it even."

"Done."

She had trotted out of Minot Air Force Base with what she needed and felt good about her prospects. That had been yesterday. Now, looking over her land and her house filled with men she knew she'd have to kill, the task ahead filled her with dread. Still, this was her land. And she'd be damned if she'd let anybody take it from her. They'd already beat her and chased her off after catching her unprepared. She had the bruises and the cuts to prove it. But she wasn't about to let that happen again.

She urged Lightning on again, and he made his way down the pass and to the edge of the pasture. She kept to the forest that ringed her land, wanting to stay hidden until the last possible moment.

As she approached the house, she could see their old beat-up truck parked by the barn. And next to it lay one of her last remaining head of cattle. As she grew closer, she could see they had only cut sections off of the dead animal that would give them the best cuts of meat. The rest they had left for later. The cold would keep it from rotting for a while, but it sure seemed a waste of a good cow.

So far, she hadn't seen a single soul and the fact that they had gorged themselves on steak and whatever else they had found in the house—whiskey—she felt for sure they were passed out. Good. That would make her plan easier.

She brought Lightning up behind the barn and tied him to a post. She went into the barn and found one of his blankets she used to keep him warm at night and flung it over her shoulder. She crept to the big tree that grew at the back of the house and started to climb it. She remembered it being a lot easier the last time she had scaled the tree. Of course, that had been when she was a little girl.

At the roof line, she stepped quietly to the shingles and crept across the roof hoping that her steps couldn't be heard below. She reached the chimney, the gray smoke rising out of it into the morning sky. She covered the chimney with the blanket and crept back to the tree, climbing down and rushing back to the barn where she positioned herself behind the water trough. She waited.

It didn't take long. A voice rose up from inside, cursing, and shouting, and then she could hear coughing and retching. The first of the brothers burst out of the back door, smoke billowing out of the door behind him. He was wearing only a pair of skivvies. The second brother followed behind the first, and they both leaned on their knees coughing. Christa sited down the M4 and pulled the trigger. The report of the rifle echoed across the hills, and one of the brothers went down. She fired again and the second one joined the first. They did not move.

Glass shattered, and she saw the barrel of an old shotgun emerge from the window at the rear by the kitchen. Smoke billowed from within, and then the shotgun went off. She fired her M4 at the window and more glass shattered, the shotgun barrel jerking upward as an angry cry erupted from within the house. Another brother in long underwear ran from the rear door, his revolver held in one hand, and he fired it wildly. His shots were not even close, and Christa realized he had no idea where she was. She sited on him and pulled the trigger three times in rapid succession. His head exploded in a spray of bone and blood and what remained of his body flopped to the ground, the big revolver flying from his hands. She stood and moved toward the house at a run.

As she crossed the yard, a shot rang out, and she spun sideways as what felt like a brick hit her in the chest. She ignored it and straightened up, running at full speed for the back door. She burst inside, the smoke billowing out through the door and making it difficult to see in her house. She moved to the kitchen and saw the youngest brother, Seth, lying on the floor, squirming, his shotgun a few feet away. She stepped to him and pointed the M4 at his head.

"Where's Bill?"

Bill was the oldest brother and the one she'd sent to prison for breaking and entering. He was the leader of the five and the one with the biggest chip on his shoulder. She hadn't seen or heard him since the battle had begun.

"Eat shit, bitch," Seth said through clenched teeth.

She pulled the trigger and shot him in the face point blank. He grew still.

She heard a sound behind her and spun around. Bill stood with a rifle in his hands, pointed at her chest. He fired point blank, and she felt the bullet knock her backward against the counter. Her M4 erupted as her finger pulled the trigger and Bill's face grew a fist-sized hole above his nose. He died instantly, his body sagging to the floor in the doorway to the kitchen.

It was over.

Coughing from the smoke, Christa covered her mouth and pushed past Bill's body and out the back door into the fresh air. She sagged to the snow and coughed more. Blood sprayed onto the white snow in front of her, and the pain finally came. It was like she'd been hit by a mack truck and all the bones in her chest felt shattered. She moaned and sagged to the cold ground where she passed out.

HEAT.

Unbearable heat. And wetness. She opened her eyes to find her house ablaze, the roaring inferno so loud in her ears that nothing else could be heard. She sat up, her clothes soaked from the melting snow around her and pain in her chest and shoulder almost too intense to bear. She took in shallow quick breaths, trying to stand. She felt as if her hair were on fire and reached up to find it frizzy and smoking.

She got her feet underneath her and staggered back toward the barn. She stood, panting, and looked out over the ruin of her childhood home. There was no saving it. The pang of regret and anger at herself for starting the fire filled her with a remorse she hadn't felt since the death of her mother and father at the hands of the virus. Hot tears rolled down her face, and then more pain struck and bent her over. She had to get to help.

She stumbled to Lightning and got him untied. He was agitated and jumpy, the fire scaring him to the point he was on the verge of bolting off, out of control. She soothed him best she could and climbed up into the saddle, crying out in pain at the effort. Blood had soaked through her clothes and coat, and the sight of it scared her.

So much blood.

She took one last look at her life burning up in front of her eyes and then urged Lightning away and back up into the hills. She had to get to The ARK. It was her only chance to survive. But it was a day's ride. And she didn't know if she'd survive.

An hour into the ride, she began to fade in and out of consciousness, her surroundings a cold blur, and the only sounds, were her horse's hooves in the snow and her own ragged breathing. Her last conscious thought was that she was going to die. Then darkness.

She woke in a dimly lit room, bandages on her chest and an I.V. in her arm. A woman tended to her, the smile on her face comforting despite the pain she felt deep down inside her chest. She tried to speak, but nothing would come.

"You're in the infirmary," the woman said. "At The ARK. Garrett brought you in. You almost didn't make it."

"My horse? Lightning?"

"He's fine and in the stables. He saved you." The woman smiled again and then left the room.

Christa felt her eyes grow heavy and was soon asleep again. She dreamed of her old childhood home. It was a good dream.

When she woke again, she was alone, and the tears started up right away. Her last memory before passing out had been a vision of her childhood home from above, the fire that had started, after she had covered the chimney with a blanket to smoke out the assholes who had taken her ranch from her, consuming the place she had grown up in. There would be nothing left but a chimney and some darkened embers and beams. She didn't know if she'd ever return. There was nothing left for her there.

The door opened to her room, and a man entered. He wore a white lab coat and had a stethoscope around his neck.

"Hello, young lady. So glad to see you awake and doing better. It was touch and go there for a while with you. I'm Doctor Thacker and if you weren't aware you are in The ARK up in the hills of North Dakota."

"Do I have you to thank for saving me?"

"Oh, not really. I think you owe that thanks to your horse and Garrett who found you two wandering out in the snow. You would not have lasted much longer out there if Garrett hadn't found you."

"Where is this Garrett? I'd like to meet him. I don't remember a thing after leaving my home."

"He's around. I'm sure he'll come to see you soon. He's been in checking on you every day."

"How long have I been out?"

"Two days. Let's have a look at you."

He approached and pulled her sheets down to look at the bandages. He poked and prodded gently and seemed satisfied.

"You're healing well."

"How long will I need to stay in this bed?" she asked.

"You can get up and move around immediately if you'd like. Just take it easy. You lost a lot of blood, and you'll probably feel weak and shaky for a few days. Have you eaten?"

"No. I'm kind of hungry."

He nodded. "That's a good sign. I'll have my wife bring you something to eat. She's the nurse that's been taking care of you."

"I owe you, Dr. Thacker. Thank you so much."

He waved a hand at her but smiled. "You'll be back to yourself in no time. Now, I'll be in to check on you again daily until we can release you. I should think you'd be good to get out of this room in two more days."

She nodded, smiling back. A knock on the door surprised

her, and it opened to a man in his mid-thirties, with sandy blond hair and slate gray eyes. He smiled as he saw her and then noticed the doctor.

"Oh. I didn't know you were in here, Doc. I'll come back."

"No, no, Garrett. I'm all finished. Come on in, and I'll let you two talk."

He turned to Christa. "We didn't know your name, and you had no I.D. So we've been calling you Jane. I assume that is not your name."

"No. I'm Christa. Christa Flaherty."

He wrote the name down on his paperwork and looked back up. "Good to have a name for you, Christa. I'll see you again soon."

He left her alone with Garrett, and she studied him standing at the foot of her bed. He was cute and carried himself with confidence. If she had to guess, he was probably ex-military. A pilot maybe.

"Christa," he said as if tasting her name. It made her feel good—and uncomfortable all at the same time. "Good to finally know your real name. Jane wasn't working for me. Christa suits you much better. I like it."

"I understand I owe you my life. Thank you."

"Your horse is the one you owe thanks. He trotted right up to me on the trail. Scared the crap out of me. He just stood there breathing steam in the cold with you on his back. He let me walk right up and take his reigns. I think he likes me."

Christa smiled. "He's kind of a pushover. But, really. Thank you. I was trying to get here on my own, but I must have given out."

"Being shot in the chest and shoulder will do that to you. You owe me that story when you're up for it. Not too often I run into a pretty girl who's been shot." He grinned.

She couldn't help it. She felt herself smiling despite the fact that he was coming on to her even in this hospital bed.

She'd only known him for a few minutes, but she liked him already.

"Deal. It's kinda boring, but I do owe you an explanation."

An awkward silence settled over them and then he cleared his throat. "So, you want something to eat? I can grab you a bite from the cafeteria, or you can try your luck at the food they have here. A little hint, the food in this infirmary tastes like glue."

She chuckled and then winced as pain shot through her chest. She reached up and touched her bandages.

"Oh, damn. I made you laugh. I guess that's not a good idea." He still smiled at his humor.

"I'm starved," she said. "I'll take anything."

"We have venison stew or venison steaks."

"The stew. How about any bread?"

"I'll grab you some if they have it. Be right back."

He left her alone, and she stared at the closed door where he'd been a second before. She guessed she could have been saved by some jerk or left for dead out there by someone who didn't care, so she was glad that Garrett had come into her life when he had.

When he returned, he was carrying a tray with a bowl of wonderful-smelling stuff and a plate that had a big hunk of bread on it. He had also brought her a glass of tea, unsweetened. He set her up with her cart and tray and then took a seat in the only chair in the room.

"You're not eating?" she asked. "You're just gonna sit there and watch me eat?"

"I could leave."

"No. It just makes me feel weird."

He stood, turned the chair around, and sat back down facing the wall. "Better?"

She shook her head. "No."

He spun the chair around and faced her again. "If it makes

you uncomfortable with me in here, I'll leave. It's all right, you won't offend me. We don't really know each other that well, but I was hoping to change that and learn a little more about the mystery woman on the horse."

She smiled, picked up her spoon, and tasted the stew. It was good. Very good. She ate a couple of spoonfuls and then took a bite of the bread. It was good too. The best she'd had in a long time.

Finally, she said, "So, what do you want to know?"

"Why were you all by yourself out there on the mountain?"

"With bullet wounds in me?"

"Yep."

"The short story is some men in my town took the liberty of stealing my house out from underneath me. I wanted it back. So I took it back. They got a couple lucky shots in."

"They got the best of you. I'm sorry."

"They're dead."

He looked surprised. "How many of them?"

"Five."

"Sounds like you can take care of yourself."

"I'm the Sheriff in the town. I know my way around a gun. Didn't keep me from getting shot, though."

"The mystery woman is a cop. Hmmm."

"Are you threatened?"

"No. Just unexpected. I'm kind of impressed."

She smiled at him and took a few more bites. When she was out of this hospital bed, she'd have to get to know this man better. Definitely.

19

Michalla felt her stomach tighten as Dr. Thacker touched her skin with the transducer.

The picture on the screen immediately showed her baby growing inside her. At seven months, the fetus had all the features of a full-grown infant, just smaller.

"Do you want to know the sex?" Dr. Thacker asked.

"You keep asking me."

"Just making sure you haven't changed your mind."

She glanced at Marty who raised an eyebrow at her. She really wanted to know but was afraid. What if it were a boy? Would she be able to handle it? She knew that eventually her fear would become a reality and she'd know one way or another whether she was having a little Ratman or a beautiful little girl. She decided it was time.

"Okay, Doctor. I want to know."

"Are you sure?"

She hesitated. And then nodded.

"It's a girl."

The relief she felt was immediate, and she felt tears well up in her eyes. Her lip quivered, and Marty reached out to grab her hand.

"Hey. It's okay. It will be okay," he said. "You wanted a girl, right?"

She nodded. "Yes," she breathed. "Yes."

Dr. Thacker removed the transducer from her belly and wiped the gel off of her skin with a towel. He shut the machine off and sat down on the little rolling stool that he used in the exam room. He seemed agitated about something but waited for Michalla to get control of herself.

"What is it?" Michalla asked, worried, now, that something was wrong with the baby.

"This won't be easy, so I'll just come out with it. With the discovery of my son's 'issues,' I'm concerned about what might develop with your child. With those concerns, I would like to run some tests on you and the fetus. Just to rule out some things."

"What kind of tests?" Michalla asked.

The issues with Dr. Thacker's son had been a big deal in the community of The ARK. The death of the mechanic six weeks ago had been a mystery for days until it was discovered that a child had committed the horrendous act. Dr. Thacker's child. His son, Charlie. An eight-year-old boy.

What would have caused a boy so young to commit such a heinous act? That had been the question on everyone's mind. And when the answer came out, Michalla, A J, Harlee, and Marty became objects of concern. The antidote that Dr. Thacker had given them all, including his wife and boy, Charlie, had been found to have some adverse reactions in subjects of a young age. Specifically, eight years and younger. The antidote caused unusually high levels of testosterone to build in the bloodstream and induce levels of aggression and anger that were abnormal. Charlie had been saved by the antidote to the virus but had been turned into a kind of monster.

He was now a prisoner of his father's own lab, a guinea pig to be studied by him and kept under close supervision. Possibly for the rest of his life.

"I want to perform an amniocentesis and take some needle biopsies of the fetus."

"No."

Dr. Thacker looked uncomfortable. He cleared his throat. "Michalla, it won't hurt the fetus. I've performed hundreds of them without injury or any complications."

"What part of my baby do you want to stick a needle into?"

He hesitated. "The brain."

She pulled down her shirt and got up from the exam table. "No. Definitely not. I won't allow you to stick a needle into my daughter's brain. No."

She could see Marty getting worked up as well and was glad that he would be on her side.

"That's crazy, Doc," Marty said. "There has to be another way. I understand your concerns. We understand your concerns, but we won't allow you to use our unborn child as a guinea pig in your sick research."

Dr. Thacker held up his hands. "I know you're upset. I get it. I feel what you are going through. I'm going through it with my own son. But it's for the best. We have to know how this antidote is going to affect future generations. Is it a viable solution or does it need to be abandoned?"

"You'll have to find someone else to perform your experiments on, Doc," Michalla said. "I won't have it."

Dr. Thacker's face changed, and his posture become tenser. "You have no choice, Michalla. The powers that be have dictated it to me. As long as you remain in The ARK, you will have to submit to whatever is necessary."

Michalla felt her mouth drop open, and she closed it slowly. "Then, we'll leave. Come on, Marty."

She grabbed his arm and pulled on him as she headed for the door.

"It is your right," Dr. Thacker said to her back. "But I'd strongly urge you to stay where you can receive the proper care. Should you need it."

"Bullshit," Michalla said.

"Just think about it," Dr. Thacker said.

She stormed out of the room pulling Marty along and made her way down the hall. She could feel the heat in her face as the anger built at the higher-ups running the show in this community. She would not allow anyone else to touch her or her baby. No one. They were leaving. Like yesterday. She wouldn't stay another second in this place.

CHRISTA STOOD outside in the crisp morning air and felt the sun on her face. Spring was the best time in the hills, and though there were still patches of snow on the ground, most of it had melted, and green was peeking up through the brown.

Her chest felt good. Not great, but good after two weeks of healing and she was glad for the expert hands of Dr. Thacker and his wife. She had spent most of her convalescence inside the dreary space of The ARK and had finally found the way outside only a few days before. She couldn't stand to be cooped up; the outdoors, something that had called to her since her youth. And for that reason, she knew she had to leave.

And it was time.

Lightning was growing restless. She had been visiting him every day now for the past few days, and she sensed his growing desire to get out into the world. She knew how he felt.

Home was not an option. That place had been destroyed, and the thought of trying to rebuild it herself was something that made her feel tired. It would always be hers. The land, the barn, the ranch. But the house was beyond repair, and for that, she knew she wanted to move on.

West. That's what was calling to her. The west. And Garrett Bourne. She smiled thinking about him. He had become somebody in her life that was important. She knew that to say she had fallen in love with him in only a few short weeks was insane, but down deep, she felt more than just a kinship with him. She didn't want to admit it to herself out loud, but in that deep place in her heart, she knew it was something special with him.

And he was leaving.

His family was waiting for him in California. A mother and brother. At least he hoped they were. But he could not stay here any longer. The few months since his plane had quit on him and he'd been forced to live in the ARK had been an experiment in his life. One he would not like to repeat.

And so, he had convinced her to go with him. It hadn't been hard. He'd asked, and she'd said she would go.

Garrett emerged from within the entrance and adjusted his pack on his back. He smiled and waved at her, and she waved back, Lightning's reigns held in her hand. The horse snorted next to her, and she patted his sides, feeling the strength of him beneath her fingers. She felt exhilarated. Excited to start this new journey with him.

"Are you ready?" Garrett asked, smiling.

"Yes. It's a beautiful morning. And I can tell it will be the best day."

"Feels good to be out of there, doesn't it?"

She nodded. He sighed, took a deep breath, and pointed in the general direction of west.

"Let's do this."

She took one last look at the entrance to The ARK and felt confident that this decision was a good one. Life was different now, and she intended to make the best of it.

She fell in step with Garrett—Lightning trotting along behind them—and took his hand in hers. He clasped it tightly, and they moved down the path, the west beckoning to them in the early morning light.

MICHALLA LED THE WAY OUTSIDE, the morning bright and clear and crisp. She felt the baby kick beneath her coat, and she reached under and rubbed her rounded stomach. Was she making the right choice? Heading out into the unknown with a baby on the way? How would she manage? How hard was it going to be traveling on foot this late in her pregnancy?

She shook her head. It would have to work out. There was no way she was staying. Not under the circumstances.

Marty adjusted his pack and smiled down at her. He seemed in good spirits. For the longest time, Michalla had known that he hadn't wanted to stay here. He disliked being cooped up under all that rock. The caves and caverns of The ARK were a place that made him feel trapped.

A J came up, still limping slightly on his leg, but ready for what lay ahead. He held Harlee's hand in his, her eyes wide and bright and full of anxious excitement at what lay ahead.

When Michalla had gone to them immediately after the visit with Dr. Thacker, they had both blurted out that they wanted to go even before she could say the words. And Michalla had cried and hugged them both. They were like family to her, and though she would have left them here if they wanted to stay, she would have missed them so much that it would have hurt.

"Look," A J pointed. "Isn't that Garrett and the horse lady?"

Michalla could see them up ahead on the path, Garrett's shape easily recognizable in the morning light. She'd only met the woman once, but had a good feeling about her. It looked like they were heading in the same direction that they were.

"Garrett said they were leaving soon," Michalla said. "I guess it was today."

"Looks like we'll have some travel companions," Marty said, and Michalla looked up at him. She couldn't read his thoughts, but if she were to guess, he was probably not keen on traveling with Garrett. The two of them had a kind of strained relationship, but over the weeks, things improved when Garrett had no longer pursued Michalla.

Michalla picked up her backpack and slipped it onto her shoulders. The weight was more than she liked, but it felt good on her back. A sign that what they were doing was right.

She stepped out onto the path and led the way west.

A direction that would forever change her.

It's over, and I know you're dying for more. The next book in *The Last Dawn* series will hit the stores very soon. You can expect to see **The Last Dawn: Sunset** in 2023. It is available for pre-order here.

REVIEWS

OF RICHARD C HALE

Frozen Past

"Hale captures emotion, seemingly effortlessly, and in turn this created reactions from me. During this read, I experienced a spectrum of emotion—anger, fear, and heartbreak to name a few. I even found myself 'talking' to the characters more than once. When an author can elicit these reactions, I consider this a true talent."

~ Carolyn Arnold, Author of the Bestseller *Ties That Bind*

"Mr. Hale's first thriller, *Near Death*, was an excellent debut novel, but with *Frozen Past*, he's bounded to a new level of mystery and suspense. Don't let this one pass you by."

~ Chuck Barrett, Amazon Best-Selling Author of *The Toymaker*

And the general public loves Richard's novels, too:

"What a ride! Richard does a great job of keeping the reader intrigued and constantly guessing. This was my first read of this author; it won't be the last."

"In his second book, Mr. Hale has a winner."

"My body felt shell-shocked from the thrilling tension the author was able to convey in his highly charged writing. From beginning to end, Mr. Hale was able to keep me on the edge of my seat wondering what the demented, psychopathic serial killer was going to do next. I must say, this killer is one of the creepiest I've read about."

Near Death

"*Near Death* is a fast-paced, romance-laced, thought-provoking, and highly entertaining novel with an intriguing premise."
~ Author Lisette Brodey

"Blew me away! An approach I never saw coming. Well Done!!! I can't wait to read your next book."
~ Author Fred Paxton

"As I read the book, I couldn't help but think about a movie and who would play each part. I envisioned Matt Damon as Jake and Paul Giamatti as Bodey. What a fantastic read. I highly recommend it."
~ Ryan Krohn, Author of *Our Beloved Red*

And more praise from everyday readers across the country:

"Richard hooked me, pulled me in, and kept me reading till the very end!"

"It was a romp that I finished in a couple of days, and I enjoyed almost every page."

"Wow, what an awesome read. I have not come across a book I could not put down like this since *The Firm* or *A Time to Kill.* The subject and story line is very thought provoking, and the twist and turns of the story catch you off guard."

ABOUT THE AUTHOR

Richard C. Hale has worn many hats in his lifetime including greens keeper, bartender, musician, respiratory therapist, and veteran air traffic controller. His most recent role—that of beloved author of thrillers—seems to suit him best.

Drop by his website, and give him a shout. He'd love to hear from you.

Contact Richard by clicking a link:
www.richardchaleauthor.com
richard@richardchaleauthor.com

ALSO BY RICHARD C HALE

"The Camera"

"Flash Mob"

"The Sandbar"

Printed in Great Britain
by Amazon

32036899R00111